LIVE FROM
FRESNO y LOS

LIVE FROM
FRESNO y LOS

· stories ·

STEPHEN D. GUTIERREZ

BEAR STAR PRESS
2009

Bear Star Press
185 Hollow Oak Drive
Cohasset, CA 95978
www.bearstarpress.com

Book & cover design by Beth Spencer
Author photograph by Monica Michelle

ISBN: 978-0-9793745-3-1
Library of Congress Control Number: 2008943328

ACKNOWLEDGMENTS

Grateful acknowledgment is made to the editors of the following journals where these stories first appeared, in sometimes different versions:

Fiction: "Just Everything" and "Feeding the People" and "Chato's Day"
Fourteen Hills: "La Gloria Meets La Helen en la Marqueta and What Is Best Left Unsaid Is for You"
The November 3rd Club: "Freddy Fender in Commerce"
Paterson Literary Review: "The Barbershop"
Santa Monica Review: "Harold, All American" and "Lucky Guys"

Red Wing Press published an earlier version of "The Barbershop" in a chapbook edition. Gracias a Quinton Duval. FC2 reprinted "La Gloria Meets La Helen en la Marqueta and What Is Best Left Unsaid Is for You" in *Latino Heretics*, edited by Tony Diaz. Gracias también. Jake Fuchs always believed in me, and that helped a lot. Charles Tatum and Thomas Gelsinon gave me support as editors at *Saguaro* magazine. Finally, Jackie, Ben, Bert.

For Jim Krusoe
Editor and Writer Supreme

CONTENTS

Man has great dignity, do not imagine that he has not.

William Saroyan,
"Seventy Thousand Assyrians"

JUST EVERYTHING

So on a Thursday night Walter finds himself on a strange porch with his new friend Nadia under a moon the size of a grapefruit, making out. She called him up out of the blue (actually she always called him up on Thursday nights, and on Mondays and Tuesdays and Wednesdays too. Walter pretended he didn't like it but liked it very much) to say that she was here, in the City of Commerce, at her mom's friend's house on a street called Jillson or something.

Walter dressed up in his best Levi's and t-shirt and trucked on over there. She met him on the corner, and now they lean against the railing looking up at that moon the size and shape and color of a grapefruit in the sky. He squeezes his eyes shut and imagines himself on it, scooping out spoonfuls before he dissolves into her shoulder, biting her.

They bite each other. They lean against each other and sigh, slurp, hold tight. They nuzzle fondly in the barren part of Walter's neighborhood, where the bank jets straight up into the sky like a concrete geyser dimly lit by the ground lights, and the rushing roar of the traffic on Washington Boulevard is constant behind them.

The house is a small, wooden structure that Walter has not noticed before, tucked into a corner between the bank on one side and an alley of similar rundown houses on the other; weeds stick up out of the dirt. Vacant lots are scattered around them. Then the neighborhood proper starts, where Walter came from.

※

Her name reminded Walter of a Russian princess wrapped in furs, but she was nothing like that. "Nadia De Leon," he liked to repeat to himself when he thought of her. "Just a new girl I know."

Walter met her a couple of weeks ago at Atlantic Square Shopping Center where he was selling raffle tickets with his buddy Fernando. He and Fernando walked up and down the sidewalks talking to people but really trying to score on the chicks strolling by.

Walter didn't know what they were doing, really. But before the night got too old, three girls from the neighborhood in Monterrey Park had come up the path between Newberry's and the next row of businesses, kind of cholas, kind of not, swaggering and chewing gum and giggling.

They had make-up on and were pretty beneath it. There was the skinny one, Alicia, and her even skinnier little sister, Elisa, who might have been in junior high going into high school next year (she was so fake when he asked her outright, "How old are you? What school do you go to?"), and Nadia.

Nadia had freckles and a nice butt and ripe melons and wore just a little bit of rouge on her cheeks and that purple stuff around her eyes. She liked to laugh.

She had slight buckteeth, but Walter thought she was cute in a weird way. Her eyes shone bright, and she was already rubbing up against Walter by the night's end when the stores started closing and the lowriders, streaming down Atlantic Boulevard toward the main drag, Whittier Boulevard, slowed to a colorful crawl in front of them.

Walter sat on a planter with Nadia next to him, and Fernando and Alicia and Elisa chatting on the other side of the lush green bush, in front of Newberry's. Fernando stretched his arms out across the bench he was sitting on, like a man of the world. He still asked people going in and out of Newberry's if they wanted to buy a raffle ticket for the Maloney High carnival.

Most of them said no, because they were all hurrying on now before the store closed; it was halfway empty inside, with one or two of the aisles darkened.

But some of them stopped and dug into a purse or a pocket to find a dollar and buy the ticket. Fernando always said thank you with a courteous smile and then turned to the girls as if they were no big deal.

They were obviously absorbed in him.

They kept asking him if he had somebody.

They wore brown, ironed corduroys with a slight flare at the bottom, square-toed, soft-suede shoes and white blouses that were tight at the chest. Elisa's was a little different and she had a long key chain dangling from her belt loop nearly to her shoe. She wore slightly darker Wallabees and chewed gum with a louder snap.

Sometimes she got bored with Fernando and looked around.

Nadia bumped against Walter and said, "Guy, I hardly know you and you're already asking me for a date?"

"What?" Walter turned to her with a smile on his face. He moved his hair away from his eyes but kind of kept his hand there. He had a big nose and didn't like to face people too much.

"I said you're picking me up at what time?" She smiled widely – more like a weird goofy grin popped out of her – and then Walter got the hint and laughed and hung his head. "I don't know, about seven, tomorrow."

She kissed his cheek and said, "Okay, let's go, girls," and then the three kind-of cholas were walking up the sidewalk back home to the streets of Monterrey Park, which ran just behind Atlantic Square, on the other side of the short wall at the end of the parking lot. He could see them climb over the wall, making fun of each other with small pushes and soft slaps, and hear them laughing and shouting. Then they disappeared under the trees into their neighborhood

He got up. "Let's go, Fernando. Let's hit the road."

Fernando was already swaggering up to him with the bucket at his side.

It was a little white bucket that he kept the stubs in, pocketing the cash in his pants. He was an all right guy, his best friend. He trusted him. He trusted him for everything.

Now Walter was hooking up with Nadia close to his house. Alicia was crazy about Fernando and had been on the phone all week with Walter about him, and Walter had given her the scoop on him.

They liked each other. Alicia always cracked up as soon as Walter said that Fernando had a girlfriend in Canoga Park.

"Canoga Park," Alicia would say, unable to get around the ridiculousness of it. "What's this Canoga Park? ¿Qué Canoga?"

They couldn't get over it. Yeah, it was bullshit, but that was Fernando. He always had a girlfriend in some weird part of the city.

Nadia had called him to come here. They were sitting on the porch.

Alicia was crazy about Fernando, but that was another thing. Fernando was a ladies' man. He played the field. He had a lot of girlfriends. He said Alicia was too skinny, "Look at her butt," and that seemed to be the last word on it as he turned up the volume on the stereo in his Porsche – his dad bought him everything he wanted; he was an only kid with two cool parents – and Walter looked out the window and thought her butt was all right.

But her smile was nice. Big and bright.

She called up Walter the next night. She got his phone number from Nadia and wanted to know everything about Fernando, how he knew him, who his girlfriend was, whether he was a flirt all the time or not.

Walter sat up in his sister's bedroom talking to Alicia till his sister kicked him out. It was the only place in the house where he could get some peace and quiet. The kitchen was too noisy and the phone was full of static, but here he could stretch out on his sister's bed and, propping himself up with some big pillows, bite his nails and talk.

He felt pretty comfortable. They began to get along pretty good, calling each other every night and talking for at least two hours.

They talked about everything. Walter rubbed his foot through his sock and cracked his knuckles. Sometimes he even smelled his hand. One time he smelled his underarm pit and wondered if he was going crazy. Nobody was there; what was he doing that for?

The door to his sister's bedroom was locked with the latch she had installed a couple of years before. The room was painted pink, a pale pink, with a bright red trim on the high shelf going all the way around the room. When they first bought the house his sister said she swore one night she was lying in there by herself, reading about ghosts on her stomach on her bed, when someone touched her.

Someone grabbed her ankle.

She swore to this day.

Walter peeked out the curtain at the usual drab scene. The Corrales house shone best. It was a nice place on the corner with a huge front window and a sharp wrought-iron fence. It was done in swirly stucco that was the new style in Commerce.

Walter's house was a stupid orangeish color with no picture window, just a narrow little one underneath a useless brown and white aluminum awning his mother had installed the summer they moved in there.

All it did was keep the house darker.

"Huh?"

"I said did you see Fernando today?"

"Oh, yeah, I saw Fernando, he was all right."

"What was he wearing?"

"Red cords and Hushpuppies, the usual. He was already in Canoga." They both started laughing.

He pronounced it with a real Spanish accent. "*Canoga.*" Not that Fernando did, just that it was funnier that way. The full ridiculousness of the situation came home that way.

He didn't know if Alicia really liked Fernando or not, or if she was just playing games to pass the time with Walter. Like she did seem to have a crush on Fernando but not too serious if she could still laugh about Canoga.

Fernando was full of shit, but he was Walter's friend. They went everywhere together. He picked up Walter in the morning in his Porsche, a yellow 914 with a black racing stripe down the middle and a bad, across-the-windshield mirror up front, inside, up above their heads where they could see everything behind them, and zipped down Washington Boulevard between the cars and trucks to school.

Maloney High. They both went to Maloney High, the boys' Catholic school in Montebello.

They smoked big joints on the way there in the morning sometimes, and then laughed in homeroom when they saw each other in second period. They were still buzzing then. It was a crack-up.

Walter lay back on the bed with the phone on his shoulder.

In this way Walter passed the time. It was no big deal.

And the moon? It was tender and beautiful. Listen. I want to back up and cover it all now as best I can, the essential parts of this story. Break it down for you.

The moon was tender, it was tender and yellow, soft as her face floating next to me, which was freckled and cute with the small buckteeth protruding, barely protruding, sweetly.

We kissed all night, stolen nibblers and luscious swirlers in the intervals between her mother stepping out every five or ten minutes to ask where her husband, Nadia's father, was at.

She carried a wine glass and stood with it on the porch again.

But I'm getting away from the story. Basic stuff. Simple stuff. Is what I want to say.

Fernando was zipping back and forth in his Porsche, crazy Fernando, zipping back and forth as if the whole world was his and always would be. He did time in the big house when he was older for theft, larceny, and all kinds of crimes I don't know too much about, really. He's still my friend and I can't bring myself to question him too closely about the past that makes him shudder and laugh at the same time.

But let me try to get some of it down for you.

He knocked up a girl his senior year, lived at home for five years without a job because he couldn't find one that suited him (high-paying, low-demanding, prestigious) while his parents paid his child support; finally got on at a sporting goods store, ripped them off, moved, avoided the authorities and charges, heavy charges; was apprehended for further theft at another store, moved, did some small time; got involved with a bunch of jokers scouring the Central Valley for expensive farm equipment. He was arrested in Mexico for transporting stolen goods across international lines – the big bust caught him flush, with thousands of dollars in a pillow case in an Ensenada motel, two broads and a pound of reefer easing his apprehension, caught him in shades and a Lakers t-shirt sitting up in bed, toasting the world with a shot of tequila.

They burst in, man, and fucked him up good. Three Federales and an agent of the California Highway Patrol jacked him up, on the spot, tossing the babes out and ransacking his room for other incriminating evidence. "Let's go, fucker," Mr. CHP ordered him. They tortured him later in jail, the agent of the California Highway Patrol conveniently stepping outside when the gruesome stuff started, but not before a complicit nod. He beat those charges for a hefty lawyer's fee provided by his parents. His Mexican compatriots went down in court. Ended up in American prisons, exceptionally well-mannered rogues I drank a shot of brandy with in Fresno once, another story ...

He moved to Florida. He sent me postcards.

He has a big scar on his face and a winning smile and that about describes him all. It comes close to who he is. Picture a Latin lover with true suavity and heart, bold and charming.

He drove that little Porsche down into the ground, floored it like the South American playboy he was (half Mexican, half Ecuadorian) racing Formula One on the streets of LA.

I sat on the front porch with Nadia for a little while, for a couple of weeks. I really liked her but was too shy to pursue it seriously. I was ugly, thought I was ugly anyway because of the way other girls reacted to me (I must have been ugly, I was ugly!) and was terribly, terribly shy around girls in those days, but I hugged her, kissed her on her mother's friend's porch that night.

I remember it was a weird thing, seeing my neighborhood from that angle. I was visiting in a part I wasn't used to, towards the back of the tract we lived in, where the houses got shabbier, the ones built before the tract went up, and right under the looming bank with the rush and roar of Washington Boulevard in our ears all night.

Our tongues met, swirled and lashed.

I touched her pussy through her tight Levi's, and she spread her legs for a moment and said, "Ai, Walter," before clamping them tight and capturing my hand between them.

We laughed softly. We kidded each other and punched our arms. On the hard concrete, we lay on our backs and looked up at the stars beyond the porch roof. They were tiny and sparkling.

God existed.

Other girls in my life didn't. Those fantasy angels could die.

Loose ends must be tied up, even as I own a big hard-on in this story, the most important element in it: that and a wet cunt, and the terrible time we wasted in those days, Nadia and me. We should've got it on behind the house in the garden under the flowering tree. We should have found a way.

We should have known each other under the moon's soft yellow light.

But we didn't.

The two other kind-of cholas were beautiful girls. I wish I could say more about them but can't. I can't remember much after the long passage of years. Alicia would call me up, Elisa would get on the phone, and we would crack up all night talking about this and that, Bobby, their next door neighbor who went to *our school too and played on the basketball team – a star, but shy; they liked him too – Fernando, me, our dog barking outside, the whole night crazy with sights and sounds intruding on my bedroom, my sister's bedroom, my sister pacing the hall wanting to talk to her boyfriend, rushing outside to meet him at the corner instead. A yellow moon waxing over the trees above her, waning – what's the difference when you're young and you got the whole world in front of you?*

HAROLD, ALL-AMERICAN

For Eric Gordillo,
my friend

Harold Lopez was a kid from East LA who moved into our neighborhood when he was about seven or eight years old; we liked him right off. He fit right into Commerce, our working class suburb down the street from his old block, the barrio he had left for our cleaner streets. We welcomed him. He was cool plus some. But he kept going to that Catholic school in East LA even as he hung around with us new dudes, us public school dudes, and kept his ways. Not really his Catholic school ways, but his ways of doing things, of being Harold. Stuck in a carpool of kids who marched at Saint Whatever It Was, a cadre of smirking nerds we tended to look down upon – salt-and-pepper-pantsed dorks when they weren't being mercenary psychopaths, weren't taking dares for a dime that jeopardized the whole city ("Climb that pole, man, and stick an M-80 in the utility box! I dare you!") – he finished his grammar school days in East LA and then bombed out on the test for the Catholic high school he should've rightly gone to. He aced most of it but failed the English part. But he was a whiz at math, really good at it, able to calculate numbers beyond our reckoning with a facility that astounded. Coupled with his athletic ability – his football stardom – his math smarts got him into the Air Force Academy at Colorado Springs.

I myself was a lost and obnoxious know-it-all in those days, with no call to say anything about it now, unless this: *I loved them, loved them all!*

And those fuckups in my town better know that ...

Harold went on to greater things. But before the glories to come, public high school I should mention, backtrack and tell you about.

Von Harold, he of the sleepy eyes and dark, white-toothed, handsome face, ended up going to the public high school where most of the kids from my neighborhood went, and I ended up going to the Catholic high school that wouldn't admit him; the opposite of him, I went from public school to Catholic school. We were always friends that way, sharing acquaintances and gossip about them in a pleasant, easy exchange that didn't disturb or bring up the fact that he had failed where I had succeeded; there was plenty of time to catch up later ...

My high school wasn't in East LA but in Montebello, a suburb nearby, where all the Catholic school kids from the area, including my own, the few who had gone to grammar school with Harold but whom I didn't want to hang around with now because they were too weird for words, went.

I came home from school and sought out my old buddies, picked up my life as though I had never disrupted it with that brash move: I was smart, I was intelligent, I was a kid of extraordinary promise, the reports said.

"Let's send him to Bishop Maloney," my mom said. "Give him a chance."

"Why not?" my dad said. "He's good for nothing around here."

So I went, donned the red and yellow jacket of the Bishop Maloney Eagles, and flung it off, took off my tie, as soon as I came home.

"Mom, I'm going to the park."

"What about your homework?" my dad said. "Why are we paying for this?"

"Leave him alone," my mom said. "He's doing good."

"Yeah, Dad," I'd say. "Leave me alone, I'm doing good."

"Knucklehead," he'd say, and send me off with a smile.

And Harold went off to Bell Gardens, of course, after me. Bell Gardens was a dilapidated town on the edge of LA, all Okie then, with a smattering of Mexicans, wetbacks and surfer types, enlivening it. It was a lot of fun going to school there, middle school, along with the rest of the kids from Commerce, every morning. On the bus, we hooted and hollered, protested our sentence to such a backward, hayseed place.

But I liked Bell Gardens. I enjoyed my years there. I met a lot of Okies, some full of fire and some just wanting to get along, some hating the world and some loving it, most of them indifferent and baffled, like the rest of us. I palled around with a few and shared some good laughs. I met a few Indians, too, wonderfully shy, quiet boys with deep pride whom I occasionally hung around with when my friends were absent, when the mood took me. And I bumped into enough Mexicans who let me know, sooner than later, that my shit stank.

"¿Pues qué traes, Chicano?" He swung around on me, fiercely, ready. "Do you think you're something?"

"Sorry, man, I didn't mean it. I was just checking out that chick over there." I pointed out a girl in line far ahead of us, a blond girl I had a crush on then, or maybe it was one of those brunettes I dug so heavily from my neighborhood. Either way, I stayed my distance from her, too glorious myself to make a move. "I didn't mean to bump you, man. I was just checking her out, it's cool."

He studied me carefully. "Órale." He extended his hand, tilting his chin up, proudly, letting me know I wasn't shit to his toughness, to his dignity, which was real, after all, and strong.

"Órale," I said back, lamely, in my own Mexican-American-style Spanish – caló, slang – not having the intonation or accent to make it authentic.

It was just a weak effort at solidarity, if sincere. It was real. He was me and I was him, if you could see, clearly, the closeness. I felt it, glimpsed it, discerned it beneath the outward trappings of our clothes and hair – his short, and mine long, a burden constantly swished out of my eyes, like a goddamn surfer's, but still mine, a Chicano head of hair, split down the middle, and black – and moved toward it, embraced it, wanted it, even as our friends denied it and knocked it down.

"Who was that wetback, man?" a friend sneered, sidling up next to me. A regular guy from my neighborhood who thought we should stick together, we Mexican-Americans, as our parents called us, or Chicanos, if they were bold enough. But they weren't, except for the few attending East LA College at night, politicized radicals feeding their kids' minds between the burritos and tacos at dinner, the hamburgers at lunch, the Santana and Motown and rock and mariachi and Edie Gorme medley of sounds coming from their credit-bought stereos with the big TV screen plunked square in the middle. Mostly they called us Mexican-Americans and left it at that.

"He was just a TJ, man, some wetback," I said, not loudly, watching him scoot up the line and load his tray with the standard subsidized lunch.

Unembarrassed, he took his orange card out at the cashier's, casually, proudly almost, as if he had nothing to hide, nothing to be ashamed of.

"Look at him, fucking wetback with a green card."

"That's an orange card, man, for lunch."

"Same shit," my friend said. "Wetback, TJ."

"Your mother's a wetback," I said.

"What?"

"You heard me."

He backed off, because he knew I had a little reputation for craziness in a pinch, wouldn't say what I couldn't back up, with fists, if necessary. Wouldn't talk shit.

"Fuck you, Frank," he said, under his breath, a sidelong glance to cool us down, to let me know it wasn't serious, his threat, his words, his empty, meaningless words.

"You're full of shit, Frank," he said, badgering me, unafraid now as we moved up in line and calmed.

We reached the cashier. "Seventy cents, please."

"Got a dime you could lend me?"

"No. Here." Always staking each other the extra quarter or nickel needed to complete a meal, sometimes one of us – the really poor of us, those without a daily dollar to spend, whose fathers claimed back injuries or blamed the Japs for stealing their jobs, not to mention the goddamn fucking Jews – digging out the orange card himself.

We made fun of these welfare guys, but not in public anymore, as we did back home in Commerce, in elementary school, when there was nobody but us to watch, to witness our disgrace.

"Here, man, have a dime and forget about it."

We were among strangers now, on our own. We had to be cool ourselves, like everybody else, and act regular, normal, rich, as if none of the Okies ever had to pull out the orange cards, tattered and torn, for a hot meal and milk. As if any of us were better than the rest.

My friend sat down next to me at a picnic table. "You're full of shit, man," he continued, "and one of these days you're gonna know it." He blasted me, getting those last words in, for some reason, as I greeted a tall, gangly Okie making his way toward us. Behind us at the table we hogged, a group of TJs loitered near the trash bins.

"Billy, my man!"

"Frankie, my boy!" We exchanged middle school inanities, and then my friend, biting into a taco, muttered words of disgust. But I was already too busy involving myself in the crowds of new people swarming over the blacktop. I couldn't pay him much mind.

I concentrated on the far dim future. Distantly gray as it was, it brightened when I imagined it, assumed a perfection unknown to us sitting among wetbacks and mangy Okies. In time, perhaps, I could be better than them, better than myself, even, whoever I was.

"You're all a bunch of pussies. You let the Okies run over you." Harold caught up with us at the park. "You're all afraid of them, man. Embarrassed or something." He was hanging his head down himself, barely letting out the words, as if they might come back to haunt him, ghost of himself that he was. "You're scared and dumb."

We were sitting under the lights at the basketball courts, headquarters for the boys.

"Naw, man, what are you talking about," somebody said. "We're cool."

"We're all cool," another guy added.

"You're all fucked," Harold said, sweeping me in with the guys he was talking about, the guys who went to Bell Gardens High now, "and sissies. You got no pride, man, you ain't got no pride." He lapsed into thick dialect.

"You're all a bunch of fucking pussies, ey," he near-shouted, leaning back as he got more and more pissed. He curved into the formal slouch of the cholo, inspecting the line in front of him as if he were a drill sergeant.

We fidgeted on the bench.

"Weak, ése," he pointed his chin at each one of us.

I cleared my throat. Then he said, "What?" and broke into that laughter we expected at such charades.

But he did say the truth. We were scared.

Nobody around us could voice it like him. He spoke what I only thought alone at night in my bedroom. A list of concerns spooled out in my head. It was like a roll call of all the people I knew and might be, all the identities inculcated in me from one source or another since birth. On and on it went, my eyes closed, breath measured, contained. Oh, I was just okay, lying down in my bed.

Wetbacks, TJs, Mexicans, Okies, Americans, whites, surfers, cholos, hippies, Chicanos, regular guys, girls, cholas, Chicanas, big-titted and fine, so alluring with those damn eyes looking me up and down at Kmart. That damn wet spot under my leg. Gotta clean up. Gotta connect. Gotta find a set that's right for me. I'm leaving the group, drifting away. But who are my friends? Those guys hanging around outside? Waiting for me at the park? They'll dump me in a second. Harold, so bold and good – he is good, he is good! – so crazy and out of touch, doesn't know a damn thing about Bell Gardens or whites, but why am I worrying about this anyway when I got a test tomorrow?

But I did worry about it. I couldn't separate myself from my friends. I felt a part of their drama wherever it played out. And news of Harold's doings, of his progress at Bell Gardens High School, meant something to me, inspired me in a way nothing else did.

He said, "Those fucking wetbacks are our friends, man!" And a flicker of understanding passed through each of us, standing around the weight room at the far end of the park, deliberating after school.

"We should be taking care of each other, man, not fighting," he emphasized, mentioning an incident that had taken place between a Chicano and a TJ that had almost turned into blows.

"Hey, and Dale Butcher, that fucking Okie asshole, he's gotta back off, man. I'm getting sick of it," Ernie, the twerp among us, shouted.

"What?" Harold came strong at Ernie, as if it were he himself being challenged by Dale Butcher right now.

"Yeah, man, he always comes up to me and knocks my hat off, calls me wetback and shit and pushes me around," Ernie leaked the news out, diffidently emboldened. Harold said nothing, just stared beyond his head at the sign on the wall, COMMERCE WEIGHT ROOM.

"Commerce, y que?" He threw it out for us, let the challenge hang in the air, as if a place name sung right established it as a true *barrio*, and were we in?

"Cut that shit out," I said, referring to the whole act.

He glared at me.

I kept up with him. I knew what was going on. I knew what he was doing.

He went into school ready, not so much combative as unafraid, accompanying Ernie, after lunch, into the hall – the cornbread corridor. There, the big bad Okies hung out, Dale Butcher among them, the meanest and craziest of the lot, liable to kick your ass for the morning workout it was, a good thrashing of a Mexican. Always in trouble with somebody, an Indian or a Mexican calling his bluff, never still, likely destined for juvenile hall and then the rest, jail and prison, Dale Butcher commanded respect early on. In those middle school years, we backed off from him and his cronies, kept away from them in careful circumnavigation of the spots they'd be at, spitting tobacco and cursing, rank rednecks with every cause to hate the world. Dale Butcher was their leader.

He ran the show. He orchestrated the medley of insults his friends used against us our first year there in Bell Gardens, throwing new ones at us to keep us current: "Wetback, greaser, spic, taco bender, Mexican," as if that were enough to rest his case.

We were inferior, naturally and undeniably inferior, because we were Mexican. Chicano. It didn't matter to him at all.

"Wetbacks" curled out of his mouth, and a jet stream of spit after a wicked snarl settled it for a slow-to-learn lackey not convinced yet, hanging around with a damn beaner or – goddamn, send in the fire department – kissing one in the hall after school.

"Whyn't you kiss a dog instead? 's got better breath."

Dale Butcher was the worst. He and his friends scared us silly, causing us to avoid them on those days when our schedules crossed. We stayed away from them, if we could, wretched Okies that snorted fire, mangy, black-toothed losers hanging out by the trash bins on their side of the school, away from the Mexicans and the Indians and any other foreigners dusking up their view. Away from us.

"Chicano," I even heard him sneer it out. "What's that? A watered-down Mexican with papers?"

Guffaws. Chuckles. Snorts. Dale Butcher and his tawdry long-haired crew kept us at bay.

"Don't go that way, man. It's trouble."

I stayed away from them, too, not because I was scared of them, particularly, but because I sensed, I think, that I had something like their own innards grinding away inside me, some feverish maladjustment working hard to keep me going but overloaded. In the right circumstance it might blow up and turn me against them. Reconstitute me into a fierce fighting machine out for blood. Enrage me with their own fury pent up and dangerous. Turn me berserk. I kept on, walking past them fast when I had to, ignoring them. And I noticed they averted their eyes as I sailed by, unless some bigger dude, monstrously tall and impossible to take on, stood in my way. I walked around him and heard his insults like all the rest of my friends.

I hated them. I could remember the worst bearing down on us, terrorizing us for the wimps we were, us guys from Commerce. They were tougher than us, really, and certainly a notch lower than us on the economic scale, slightly more barbaric – as if any of us were barbaric at all. I can finally see that now. I can see clearly what has been hidden from me, in a bottle, for years.

Harold went to school the next day and protected Ernie. He walked down the hall with him, staring down the mean Okies lining the walls, breezing by them with emphatic confidence, strutting almost, just shy of mocking them. He wore Ernie's cap and locked eyes with Butcher for the split second it took to pass him, Butcher looking away and Harold patting Ernie on the back into his classroom, seeing him safely in. Just another day in the life of the man.

"Harold's a hero," I said. "I told you he was bad."

"Aw, shut up," Harold said. "Leave me alone."

"Okay," I said. "Have it your way." But he was chuckling himself.

"Now everything's different, man," somebody said.

"Yeah."

"No more bullshit from any of the fucking Okies, man, it's all good now," another guy threw in.

Everything changed after Harold's bravery, which seemed less bravery than common sense, Harold at work – inevitability. He cleared a path for them. Now, instead of shyly avoiding the spots where they might run into the toughest Okies, they walked anywhere they pleased with swaggering simplicity, Harold leading the way.

Harold said, "Aw, man, it's no big deal, it's not a big thing."

But I knew it was. Anything to make anybody feel safe was good. Harold had accomplished the impossible for them, free passage through the halls of Bell Gardens.

And I rejoiced with them, gloating over the fact of Dale Butcher humbled. Made to eat a little crow. Served up with salsa. Picante. Á la Harold. But it was only a matter of time before Butcher met his match, I often thought. There were some bad motherfuckers going around LA, as there are now, seasoned vatos fresh out of the joint with nothing to lose and a whole lot to prove, if you slighted them, if you doubted them.

I edged away from them, always, created a space between us when I found myself standing next to a bona fide cholo at the hamburger stand or taquería deep in Los, too close to a killing vato with the tattoos and scars and sewn-up bullet holes. I always did so with a lot of respect, though, a lot of admiration even, for those who would live what they believed, no matter how twisted and tormented their creed.

I said, "Dispensa," and got in return the sign of brotherhood in the quick nod and grunt from a vato waiting for his order. I approved of them, in a way, as if their hallucinatory image was the only real one in a landscape of subterfuge.

But not everyone agreed.

My mom said, "They are embarrassing, an embarrassment to the human race, to all of us Mexican-Americans. In our days, pachucos were stylish. But now, poof," she indicated with a flash of her hand. "Nothing. Verdad, Frank?"

"I don't know, I forget."

Harold's mom must have said the same thing, because she warned him against us, even: "Watch out with those boys, Harold. They're trouble."

He told me this later when he was bitching about her.

"Cuidado, they haven't had the upbringing you've had. They're," she whispered the word, "Chicanos."

"What do you think I am?"

She looked at him for the first time as if she didn't know him.

My dad sat in his armchair. He said, "Give me a beer, son. Tell me how you're doing in school."

"I don't know, I'm class president."

"Really?"

"Really."

"Wow." He lifted the empty to his lips, put it down on the end table next to him. "Virginia, why didn't you tell me about this? What do you think, I'm – "

"Sordo? Yes, sordo," she said, pointing to her ear. "You don't hear these things. You don't remember them."

"I forget," he cleared his ear of wax. "Speak up. Do something!"

"I'm trying, Dad."

"I know you are, son," he said. "That's all you can do in this world, just try. Do something! And show them your balls when you're in a pinch. Fight back until it's over. Then walk away, too, like a man." Then my dad bent his head down and wiped his cheek. Something was shining.

Harold got himself an audience. TJs gathered around him for help with their homework. Harold gladly worked with them on their math problems, bending heads with resourceful TJs as good at math as he was. They just challenged each other. But when it came to English, they all stank.

But he could do other things for them, the TJs. He could argue with the grouchy old seamstress who refused to take their money for the soccer uniforms because they couldn't speak English, turning her sour face up when they timidly suggested this could be real easy, real simple, if she'd just let them pay and walk out with their orders.

An equivalent of "here's the money and our orders" came out in tattered patchwork English too shabby for her, and Harold came to the rescue, flying in with a Superman cape lettered, of course, H.

Harold, All-American, más loco que la chingada.

Our friends said, "C'mon, Harold, we're gonna miss the bus."

"You guys go, man," he said. "Nobody asked you to come."

Afterwards we talked about it. "Harold's going off the deep end. He's hanging around with TJs."

"Let him," I said. "He'll blend in more with you guys."

That was the ultimate insult. They called me a Catholic school baby and a coward.

I took it all in stride. "You're right," I said. "What am I doing there?"

It just wasn't done, admitting TJs.

"Well, fuck that. I'm not going to hang around with TJs."

"Nobody's asking you to, Rudy. Just get rid of those pants."

"No haw-blow español. Fucker," he said. "Smartass."

Which was true. We couldn't be Mexican even if the desire took us. We didn't have the skills.

Our Spanish was half-assed.

Harold was the only one of us who spoke Spanish, who came from a family with two Mexican parents, two Mexican brothers, a Mexican dog, and an aquarium imported from China. "Este es de china," I imagined they said, happily whole.

We professed to hate Spanish.

Harold said, "What's wrong with Spanish, man, it's cool."

"Nothing, man, everything you do is cool, Harold."

"You're full of shit, Von Frankenstein," he said.

"Yeah, but it's coming out," I lifted my leg and farted, "steadily."

This was in the eighth grade. We were sitting on the railroad tracks behind the factories. He had just failed the test to get into the high school I would go to the next year. He was disappointed, but not much. "I guess I'll go to Bell Gardens. What's out there?"

"Okies and Mexicans."

He looked at me.

"A few Indians."

"What else?"

"Girls."

He looked at me again. "Why are you going to Maloney?"

"I don't know, I just want to." That was the best answer I could give him. I wanted to try something new, stretch my mind a bit, slip into a new experience for a while. "Why?"

"Just wondering, man. Check out the chicks at St. Eugenia. They're hot."

He was right. No need to elaborate on that point. Across the street from Maloney, protected by a chain link fence that sagged at the corners, St. Eugenia All-Girls Catholic School proved my stomping grounds over the next four years. I set some records. I broke some hearts.

Harold said, "Fuck, man, be good."

"All right, I'll try."

We didn't want to be confused with TJs, is the bottom line; it was the least thing we could do, the meanest state we could fall into. We were pretty sick individuals, and I mean that.

Harold threatened us all one night.

We weren't Mexicans.

Harold knew this and laughed.

We didn't know who we were.

Harold knew exactly who he was. In his first year at Bell Gardens High he became his own man. He showed his balls.

Soy Chicano, fuck it, I still think there's something to be said for balls.

Which brings me to football, fall, and me at my desk, struggling with these words, a failed writer, however clichéd that sounds, making sense out of whatever I can. That's not much. And I go back in time, to seven or eight years ago, and a biting night, first signs of fall in the air, like tonight. I am sitting in a seminar room at an oblong table in an Ivy League hall, listening to the graduate students chatter on about my work.

"Aren't the lower classes so full of life and energy?" a gangly Princeton grad says to another woman as we gather up our materials to leave. My story has just been discussed, a tale about our doings in Commerce, about you and me, Harold, and a small run in with the law that turned out well. Luckless doings of two guys in the 'hood, caught in amorous hijinks with two girls and enough pot to act big, laughing off their escapades in tempered Chicano slang. It was from Commerce, after all, not Los.

So the other woman says, Harold, listen to this, she says, "Yes, I love the lower classes, especially Mexicans! They're so colorful!"

Harold, All-American, lend me a hand. I walked outside into the night. The swaying leaves were sad things under the trees, hanging off the branches.

I shook and shuddered all the way home, and wrote no more.

And now, Harold, what do you call me? A bigger fool than you? A simpering, idiotic sissy? You with your own story of failure and displacement, emptying out and refilling.

Harold, mi amigo, I'll write both our stories. I await the muse in the driveway of my suburban house in Fresno, taking in the night. Cold, brisk, starry, this Valley town does something for me. Seven years later, annoyed and bitten, reading the magazines of the successful, of the made-it, I say, "Fuck it, they're so bad. Nothing in there I can't do, that's for sure." Nothing in this town holding me back; got a job, a girl, a car with good tires and 60,000 miles, hell, I got it made, I'm doing all right. I'll make it all right, Harold, watch me.

Watch me and listen. There is so much to say, wanting to come out now, wanting to live. There is something in the air, the thin fall air, making me want to rise and speak my story, my dreadful story.

Harold, All-American, pry open my mouth, force out my words. Your shoulder-lowered booms on the high school football fields fill me with wonder; your badness, your fearsomeness, hitting somebody, hard, yet to be spoken of.

Scanning the night sky for crisscrossing American jets, ready to record this tale of rare fuel spent and plenty more to use, I am down here on the ground with you, looking up, and only our locura makes sense.

HAROLD, ALL-AMERICAN
más loco que la chingada
or
A Short and Sweet History of a Chicano
With No Softness in Him but Goodness
No Badness in Him but Justice
Who Had a Good Mathematical Mind
But Couldn't Write an Essay Worth Shit

So what? I'll write it for you, brother, take over for you from here on out, no longer fuck around with those wastrels my demons, but explode, instead, on the page:

HAROLD, ALL-AMERICAN
The Craziest Motherfucker Around
Whose Story Is My Task

Observe. Ghosts rise off the fields of your triumphs. The Bell Gardens Lancers' cheerleaders perform a dance just for you, kicking high in unison, reaching the stars in soft-tipped tennis shoes, coming down to the ground together, clapping, slapping their hips to this beat: "Here we go, BG! Here we go!"

I still have no inkling of Harold being a football player, no sense of what he contains. But early on, in memory, this comes to me, an incident out of Cub Scouts. It happens on a tired Tuesday when we go to Den meetings at Mercy Martinez's, a pink stucco house with a pool in the back and a snotty kid lording over the snack tray. Out front, Harold's running around with his shirt untucked. It's flying out of his salt-and-pepper pants, and Harold is two steps ahead of his own fleeting image, when someone, a bigger kid in the Den, hits him.

Harold lands on his butt. He looks around. He gets up.

He brushes himself off, says, "Let's play football, dude." Next play, watching the bigger kid come at him, studying his moves, Harold corners him, lowers his shoulder, and buries him, the bigger kid crying with his hand to his chest, out of breath.

Harold stands above him. He says, "Shouldn't play rough if you don't like it."

That's the first time I saw him play football. The second time was worse.

Harold Lopez was a household name in our town by the time he finished playing for Bell Gardens High. *Want some kick-ass? We'll provide* might have been his motto in those days when he ran rampant along the line squaring off against anybody in front of him. He was bad.

Harold, All-American, let's run down your record.

"Here we go, BG! Here we go!"

First year accolades come quick. He is immortalized on page 3 of the *Commerce Tribune*, a roving photographer spying something great, I think, in that husky boy working the tackling dummies. Takes him aside and snaps him clean.

Harold, kneeling on the grass with his hand on his helmet: "Suited Up!" And I think that year he was Honorable Mention, All-League, Left Tackle.

The roving photographer comes back, seeks him out for the second-year kudos. Harold, in a crunch shot of a picture-perfect hit: "Ow!" That must've been Junior year, First Team All-League, Offensive Tackle, Second Team All-League, Nose Guard, a position he relished because he got to hit the fuckers so hard, every play!

Harold, senior year, coming into his mighty own. This picture is special. He gazes at the game from the sidelines with his coach, the coach's hand on his shoulder: "The Problem Solvers." Senior year, the year he won everything.

Harold, Extracurricular Guy, is more than a jock. These pictures are rated X, but we love them: big Harold randomly exposed in a salacious series we took in our minds, unbelievably lucky. He is no doubt caught in a blurred picture with Rosa Pimental, the head cheerleader in our town. Shy and elusive, she hardly talks to anybody without a passport from her father, an old-time Mexicano without the mostacho but with the pistola, you suspect, handy. He posts himself at the gate every night, tripping up pretenders.

"¿Hablas español?"

"No."

"¿Qué quieres?"

Harold quit the silliness. He took her out to the prom and won the bet he had consented to with a lot of laughing and swearing.

"Fuck you guys," he said, "that's my girlfriend."

"A man is a man, homes, unless he's less than a man."

"In which case he's something like a boy."

"Frank, don't get all fucking philosophical on us."

"Sporting a beard but no real hair."

"Fuck you guys, I'll do it," he said, grinning in our faces as we set terms.

"Fifty bucks."

"I've only known her three months, man."

"Long enough to know her, if you're a man."

"Shut up, Frank."

He cackled when he collected our money, draping the pliant trophy over his shoulder as if he had won a new letter in a second sport, long and hard, requiring a lot of stamina.

"Pay up, fuckers," he said, counting our crumpled bills. "It's a man's world and it takes a man to do a man's job," he continued, falling into the Mexican-accented speech we used when we wanted to make a deep point we couldn't say straight. "Un hombre, ése, para todo tiempo." He puffed his chest up and sniffed.

"Hey, these panties are too big for Rosa!" A quick hand snatched them off his shoulder and held them in the air, crotch worn, waistband wobbly.

"Since when are you a fucking expert on women's underwear, dude?" Harold grabbed the panties back and stuffed them deep in his pants pocket, along with the fifty bucks, and we cruised on over to Shakey's Pizza for a party that went down as legend because they served us beer.

"We drank all night, man. We partied till we puked."

"Yeah, you did. I could hold my liquor." In later years, we ran it all down and revised according to our needs.

They couldn't drink. I could.

"Fucking Frank. You drink too much, man, slow down."

"Fuck you."

Harold won the prize, the biggest trophy in town. Or, rather, turning out to be fully mortal, a flesh and blood woman, she consented to marry his sad ass. Rosa herself said yes. She gave him her hand, agreed to do all kinds of awful things, like sleep with him every night. She even bore his children.

She lives with him now in a snazzy new development, The Towne at Commerce. Does all that is required of her besides being beautiful and available to hear his complaints about everything from the lawn going bad to the cheap governor, not to mention the need for a good pick in the upcoming draft.

"Just to make it interesting."

She does more. She rides around town being beautiful (did I already say that?) without being obnoxious, unpleasant or, Lord forbid, a tease, and gets the kids ready for mass on Sunday, Harold staying home to flip the channels on the TV and catch a game or two in football season, without any real passion, any real investment in the outcome. He skips mass because he doesn't require it of himself, even though he's a devout Catholic, almost fanatical in his defense of the church and its beliefs.

"I don't need to go to mass, man, God's inside me whether I step in there or not." But Holy Mother Church is not to be disputed; what it pro-

fesses cannot be denied. It's the truth of the Lord brought to life, to earth
… to suffer, die and …

Harold, the up-and-coming gent, the clean-shaven guy, buys himself a
nice, three-bedroom, two-story home that, with his ingenuity and know-
how, he extends into the back yard to make yet bigger and better. It is
more capacious and luxurious. It is truly comfortable and impressive, the
new den, the dog run at the side of the house, the hot tub in the back
yard under the flowering tree, all immaculately kept. And surrounded by
neighbors as conscientious as him, neighbors who keep up their houses,
Harold is pleased. The neighborhood stays clean, maintains its value, appears prosperous, and is.

Working-class guys in managerial positions fix up old cars on weekends, play a little touch football in the fall, and invite Harold to join a
league for old time's sake.

"Just to go out there and get some exercise, man, you're getting fat."

"No, I'm not." He pinches a roll of flesh. "That's my proof of the good
life. Anything more is bad. For now, estoy bien."

He doesn't want to play football. It bores him.

"Why would I want to do that anymore," he tells me. "I've played my
football." On his mantel, a trophy proves him one of the best in his time.
Though unremarkable in aspect, just a small shining glob of gold with a
smaller plaque under the football, it names him to the All-Southern California team that we knew was really an All-America team. It had to be.

Harold, All-American, our friend.

He gets up in the morning and walks the dog, a sleek, gray, stubby-
tailed pointer that he paid good money for. He has hunted on occasion but
not so much recently, likes to play with the dog more than take him out in
the field. He picks up the paper from the porch and reads it inside when
he's done with the dog, flips through it over his coffee, enjoying, particularly, the financial reports and sports.

He works for Cal Trans in the office. He started on the line and got
promoted so rapidly he just about broke his neck bumping his head on the
ceiling of his grade. He's behind a desk five days a week dispatching teams
of orange-vested guys and studying projects and writing up proposals for
the work he does on the freeways around LA. He understands traffic better
than most executives above him, he confides more than complains ("Really,

it's true. It just turned out that way. These guys don't know anything"), and is bemused with the pompous experts strutting in with their brand-new college degrees. He himself has an AA from East Los Angeles Community College, not a BA, in a field called civic engineering that got him to his current position. It is well paid, secure, honored, respectable, and challenging.

He likes it. He no longer worries about bigotry, as he did in the past. Sure, there's a remnant of an old guard still a little dangerous, but mostly it's cool in the office. He's gotten where he has gotten to by sheer ability and smarts. He's reached the top by his own efforts.

"And nobody else's. I did it on my own. I visit sites and look at my work and just feel good. Really, man, I feel good when I see something I've done."

"Sure, man, and then you wake up and you're in a field naked with an overpass crashing down all around you."

"Or something like that," Harold agrees. A crumbling overpass can be attributed to his malfeasance. Every breakdown in town is his responsibility. The whole wrecked city can be blamed on him.

"Sure, man, everything."

"But at least you got insurance. Chicano Policy # ¿Donde Está mi Cheque? Get Me Out of This Fucking Zoo, Ése, Backup, ¿qué no?"

"Two of them. And you, Frank, what do you got going for you?"

"Nothing."

"You lie, man. You wait and see."

"Okay, man, I'm waiting."

We sit under the elaborate patio lights in his back yard, bullshitting. Two or three of us have converged from points not too far off to check in with Harold. He brings out the beers and passes them around generously. He cracks us up, tells us old stories we've forgotten the endings of because we didn't listen closely enough the first time, but always leaves out the one that matters, the one that counts.

It was September in our freshman year of high school. September, with the scant trees shedding yellow leaves, thin reminders that LA did have seasons, and the summer heat absconded. Only our own heat left in the air, lingering behind us. Effluent and musky. A new year in a new school, and all the girls wanting it, badly, even the good girls at St. Eugenia, oh yeah.

We tripped along the park's paths.

"Did you hear about Abel?"

"What?"

"He got down with Martha."

"Bullshit."

"Who told you that?"

"Abel."

"Bullshit."

"If only I could …" We stopped short, held ourselves in tightly, and waited for the courage that might permit a real confession.

"What? If only you could …"

"See yo' mama naked!"

But we knew they wanted us. With just a little coaxing we could get them here, in our arms, in no time. In the next few months, plenty of girls would lose their innocence, their flirtatious smiles turning into deeply gratified moans of pleasure under our caresses. We would break them down. We would fuck them hard.

Nothing could hold us back. We had a plan.

It started with a smaller plan that would get them in time.

"Mom, I'm going to the park."

"Don't stay out too late, your dad's sick and needs a rest."

"Again?"

"He's tired only and needs to sleep. He stays up for you."

"Okay."

But it never panned out. We had ourselves. Some of those appointed nights we spent watching basketball games, off in our usual spot in the corner of the park, the courts busy with the huffing, puffing men who came in during their lunch hours to play.

They were businessmen, engineers and executives from the neighboring factories, probably working nights to save their companies in hard times. They played fiercely, determinedly. They ranged over the courts with impunity, as if they owned them. Athletes, jocks, competitors shouted out frenzied advice. "Pick him up, Bob! Use your body!" No-nonsense captains of industry showed what the game was about. They took for granted their exalted positions on the earth, on top of the world, or at least on this lean patch in Commerce. With a basketball in hand, they drove and played to win. They couldn't stand losing.

Harold must have sniffed this out, because one night, tossing a ball up in his hand, he asked if they wanted to play us, in football. They had just started to warm up, and glanced at us all, taking in our collective challenge.

We grinned, standing behind Harold gamely.

They said, "Sure," and we walked across the court to the field. We kicked off and started playing.

Then we lined up across from each other. Harold, assuming a three-point stance opposite a graying man in sweats, exploded at the snap. He slammed into him.

The man fell, and his teammates rushed to his side to help him. "Son, you oughta be in pads," another man came out with the obvious. He led his friend off the field, scolding Harold but not angrily, more matter-of-factly, even commiseratively. Ah, to be young again and full of fire, bloodlust, and mayhem.

"You got no business here."

"Are we gonna play football or not?" Harold barked, but we knew it was time to go home, his own teammates trickling off the field in separate rivulets.

That was the second time I saw him play football.

Football. Basketball. Broads. We traded our enthusiasms for new ones. But most of the time we did nothing, swaggered on the winding paths of the park, catching the occasional soccer game to amuse ourselves. We hated soccer. It required a small white ball that you only kicked. How lame!

But it seemed right for the Mexicans playing it, bumbling fools. We stood along the sidelines making fun of them every chance we got. During warm-ups, we really laid it on, unafraid to insult them because they were just loosening up, not playing yet.

"Tch, tch, hey, TJ," we catcalled imperiously, borrowing from their own language to humiliate them, the slang itself handy. We'd heard them enough times to know it. "Pasa me the ball."

"Tch, tch."

"Where's Harold?"

"Where's that fucker?"

"I don't know, man, jacking off or something."

"You're always talking about jacking off. Let me see your hands."

"Tch, tch."

They ignored us, too absorbed and self-confident to be bothered, hard-working men staying in shape, exercising. They hit balls with their heads and did weird exercises, jumping in place and twirling their arms. They raised their knees in succession.

"There he comes, fucker."

"Look at that, man."

"Shit."

He began to cut across the park, crowned with a hat. He passed the TJs, making an effort to avoid their game, what looked like the beginning of a scrimmage bursting out, and tipped his hat to them.

The TJs sprang at us.

"Vete a la chingada," they cried.

"Chicanos. Sin nada."

September, and Harold materialized as a cholo. He stormed across the field and met us in his garb. Did this for no reason that anybody could discern, no concrete incident behind him that could explain such madness, such breaking out of the norm. He felt like it. Quería. He was bad enough to invite the disdain and fury, even the danger being a cholo meant in LA, so he did. He was Harold, Not Yet All-American but Todavía Chicano Total.

We went way back, ése, you understand? To those days in Cub Scouts lining up in the back yard in our uniforms, askew and sloppily matched, saluting the flag that flew at the school three blocks away because we didn't have a flag yet, Mercy Martinez laughing along with us, "Turn that way, boys! Turn that way! Salute the flag! Say the Pledge of Allegiance!" Nobody owned a flag in our city, except the gabachos, and the veterans, and the recipients of the Flag Day giveaway at the park attended by those future fascists of America, The Patriotic Club of Commerce members.

Nobody had a fucking flag. Nobody needed one.

Harold was a living, walking flag, waving in the faces of all those who had oppressed him. No, not oppressed, insulted. No, not insulted, proscribed the limits of.

Proscribed, I write, and laugh. Words and words and words gush up beautifully, don't they?

The chavalo, yo, was already playing with them, throwing them around in smudged essays circulated among the elementary school parents in mimeographed newsletters. *By Frank...*

Harold, All-American, más loco que la chingada...

"I pledge allegiance, to the flag," we finished up, and Mercy wiped the near-tears from her eyes, the old battle ax of the Avenues of the wild decades past getting a kick out of our flagless den, our stateless group, saying, "Frankie, you better write about this one day, you better, because I'll be goddamned if I'm not the den mother without a flag. And aquel Roy the janitor, all drunk at the school, keeping the damn thing up past three because I asked him to. Oh boy, oh boy, oh boy. ¡Ay, Dios mío! We're too much. You're going to have to remember this, Frankie, when you're older. Okay, boys, get in line! Let's go march or something!"

"Cookies! Cookies! Football!"

We went way back, Harold and I did, proudly wrapped in the royal blue of the Cub Scouts of America, yes siree, saluting Old Glory and collecting cans for orphans in the projects and knowing how to tie knots even. Square knot, bowknot, Chicano knot when you just throw everything in and pull. Laugh until your sides ache, doing some silly shit.

And Harold, forgetting the Law of the Pack (or remembering it?), bestirred himself to stand before us todo chingón. Nobody knew why. Nobody cared or even thought about it. He just stood there stunning us.

And theories flew through my head. They zipped around in the gray matter, where things fell into place in time, never at the moment you needed them to, always late, always delinquent. But even so, I must have calculated quickly the situation in front of us and assessed it: Why the fuck is Harold standing before us todo chingón?

And answered: Easy. It was something he heard, some slur slipped into his ear this morning in the lunch line by a quickly retreating Okie or even spat out by a pimply fool stupid enough to challenge him before the hall monitor broke them up. Or maybe it was the same PE teacher, now teaching at Bell Gardens High, who sneeringly addressed me as Pancho my first year at Bell Gardens Middle School, clearing his throat, glancing up from a table in the locker room impatiently, snagging the attention of a confused and disinterested Chicano already daydreaming of doing better things than waiting for a goddamn fucking locker assignment: Pancho, Pancho, Pancho. "Hey, Pancho, this way, eh?" Mr. Nelson, name unchanged, from Orange County. Idiot. Stupid.

Maybe it was worse than that, and already Harold had fought, squaring off with one of the Okie toughs at noon, scuffling by the trashcans and coming out on top, or, just possibly, the bottom, with a split lip quickly healed but a broken ego demanding restitution. Fucking Mexican, wetback. Try that again? One of these scenarios had driven him to don the uniform of the colorful, famed psychopaths of nuestra fair city, LA. Yes, you heard right, psychopaths, murdering and shooting up and otherwise having fun in LA, besides styling como querían and not giving a damn what anybody thought, having a good old time cruising on a Sunday afternoon and picking up the rucas at the parque and bang, bang, shoot 'em up, the vatos who didn't look right – "Where you from?" the three meanest words in LA – starting it all over again en la noche, ése, la vida loca, because that was the life of a a cholo, ¿tú sabes?, no other.

And we had our own stories to tell. They were of *not* becoming a cholo. Mostly from our middle school days, they ended like this: "Are you crazy, you can't go out like that!" In my case, my mother screamed of shirts hanging out dangerously uncouth, not tucked in right. "You look like a slob! A cholo!"

We stuck to our closets full of almost-attire. But we dared ourselves to shut up and put them on, khakis, official khakis. Why not show up at Bell Gardens with a warring message to any Okies scaring us into submission? They had their own style of dress, mean enough, biker dirty and Iron Cross tough.

"Why not, man? They're so bad, let's show them back."

Slip into some khakis big enough to hide a switchblade, a slick Tijuana push-button sweetly nestled in the hollows of a pocket so long you could also tote a spray can for quick and easy access. Get high, write your name, reach in and draw your filero when somebody questioned you. Fight back.

It all started with the insane pants.

"Ah, man, you wouldn't dare. You'd trip all over."

"But it'd be bad, huh? Kind of."

"Give me the money and I would, man, I swear."

"You wouldn't. Your mother would kill you."

"Still, man, I'd like to try it, just for once. Be bad."

"A todo madre. Simón."

"Where'd you learn to talk like that, man?"

"My uncle. He's in prison."

"I didn't know that."

"Nobody does."

"Why don't we do it, man?"

"Because we're chickenshit. We can't."

"Let's at least cuff our pants or something. Be Chicano. I mean *Chicano*."

"Órale."

"Frank, you can't pronounce Spanish worth shit, man. Where'd you grow up, Bell Gardens?"

"Your mother's plaza."

"Fuck you, dude."

"Órale."

"Let's cuff our pants tomorrow, man. See you at the bus stop at eight."

Chicano style. We captured it. Whatever made us different, we knew it, whether it was a minor adjustment to the pants or a shirt that announced us, or the right pair of shoes, not too surfer, not too cholo, just casual, man, Chicano, or a belt with an inscribed name without any hippy flowers, Old English letters flaring up instead, or a pair of ear muffs to ward off the winter cold ("Frank, where'd you get those from, and why? That's like the weirdest thing I've ever seen you wear." "It's the new style, dudes, you guys just haven't caught on." Shit, get my ass home into bed! Pull the blankets up to my chin and claim a fever! I'm never coming out again!), or even a t-shirt with some wild design, we stayed true to ourselves. Style, we had our own Chicano style, and clung to it.

Harold didn't give a goddamn fucking shit about what we wore and how. He said fuck it that night. He set his own standard, made his own statement, and treated our circumspection with the contempt of genius for mediocrity. He redefined style.

He looked the same as they all did, and different, and better, standing in a pair of classic khakis, creased at the top and tapering to a tighter fit at the bottom, as if in subtle tribute to the forerunners of this whole look, los pachucos. Pero khakis nonetheless, starched and baggy at the same time, under a blue Pendleton shirt as pressed and creased as the pants. It was buttoned at the neck and fell loosely around him, reminding me of nothing so much as a ballerina's dress, until I blinked and saw the dancer, scowling, mean, and the hard shoes buffed to a luster that were planted in the ground, ready to kick, lash out, run, anything but dance.

But he surprised me again. He danced – swayed, stepped forward and backward in an intricate movement inviting a response. *Let's do it, Frankie. C'mon, baby, the rest of you, too. Let's show them what heart we got, true cora, and any paddy fucker getting in our way, knock him down and beat him to death. Kill him. Stomp on him. Kick his fucking ass but good. Let's be cholo to the core, ése. Bad, fucking bad, and crazy.*

I watched him. I steadied my gaze. Silently, we moved in a circle, and the air thickened, grew disgusted with our very movements, so that I had to turn aside and say, "Where'd you get that shit from, Harold?" or somebody did.

My mind, occupied with the spectacle in front of me, refused to take part in it, but my body couldn't resist. I followed. I danced too. I became his willing partner, and every one of us dudes circling him moved to his steps, only watching him, too, his hand in his waistband, not exactly sure he wouldn't pull out a cuete. Who knew how crazy he had become? Not exactly sure he hadn't popped up for some unspoken vendetta borne of a slight that had been eating at him for days, months, years. Not exactly sure he wasn't as dangerous as he looked.

So we turned away, sighed, became our normal selves. Ha!

And those selves moved differently from Harold. We were pretty boring kids, after all, "normal," "average" working-class kids out of Southern California, barrio-tainted, maybe, suburban-influenced to some degree, certainly, ambiguous in our blue-collar backgrounds, drawing from everything around us, positively and without doubt true.

We were unglamorous Southern Californians, neither barrio nor suburban, one thing or the other, but most often mistaken for the inner city guys we really had nothing in common with.

Nothing? Little in common with? I ask myself.

Something, but less than everything.

We were Commerce kids, more specifically, Rosewood Park kids, raised in that safe corner of the Model City known by all for its fabulous swimming pools and quiet, peaceful streets that, at night, rankled no one. We ate and slept and dreamt by the freeway flowing close enough to reach all our ears constantly, and our parents got up in the morning and drove off to work sure of another glorious evening in June, sprinklers on the lawn in full rotation, buses running late to take home the kids from the other parks, helicopters hovering just that side of the Santa Ana freeway to remind us of our distance from (and proximity to) the barrio. People confused us with East LA, but we weren't.

Our parents reminded us. "This isn't East LA. Don't act like a cholo."

And we nodded our heads. Of course, there were those of us who misinterpreted the rules and created our own game plans out of the bits and pieces of what we saw around us, and ended up tragically. Those stories are awful and instructive. But this is the story of Harold, the best of us, and it takes a turn I wish I could have seen live the night it happened instead of replaying it in my head from secondhand reports.

My friends told me about it. They told it well.

"Harold almost killed somebody, man," they said. "He almost broke some big white boy's back in San Marino, up there where the rich live."

This other player, on the opposing team, couldn't accept Harold. He epitomized the difference everybody sensed in San Marino. "Even the air smells different up there," my friends said about the town on the edge of the San Gabriel Mountains. "Cleaner, better, purer."

"And worse," I said.

"Wetback, grease ball, spic." He had been bothering Harold all night, taunting him, humiliating him with loud insults, assuming his position across from him and usually getting the worst of it, so mad. When Harold told him between plays, one finger under the brute's chin, "You better stop it, man, or I'm going to get you," he laughed.

"Fucking wetback. What are you going to do? Kill me? Stab me in the alley? This isn't fucking East LA, man. This is San Marino."

"Yeah, right."

Harold got into the loose, egg-shaped huddle and was trembling. Defensively, he played the line (as he did, offensively), nose guard, but he stayed back at the snap.

"There he goes, man, there he goes," he told us later how he charted him.

"And I'm off."

Taking advantage of a full sprint, Harold met him midway up the field with a blistering hit square in his back. A flying projectile aimed its helmeted head at an opposing player looking around confusedly – the play was over and done now, #68 standing still before going back to the huddle, dimly aware, maybe, of chaos headed his way – and then gasping and arching his back before sinking to the ground and crying.

"No, no." Then what came out of him sounded like whimpers mixed with pain. Then nothing came out of him.

"Is he alive?" players asked.

"I think so. Yes."

An ambulance crept onto the field – everybody feared paralysis, the head coach frantic about no movement below – and the paramedics lifted #68 onto the gurney, slid him inside, closed the doors, and drove off the field. The red lights spun, but the siren stayed off until they hit the street and the whole crowd in the bleachers turned to watch the ambulance speed away, wailing.

"Jaysus," a friend of mine overheard an old timer in the bleachers ruminate on it all, an Okie wearing a Bell Gardens Boosters Club jacket and a Dodgers cap. "Did you see that boy go down? Did you see that boy that hit 'im? He must've been flying at ninety miles per hour, just stretched out and," he ran a fist into a palm, "wham! Laid him out. I never seen nothing like that, nothing. Must've been crazy with something. That's the only way you act that way, crazy."

Play resumed, and Harold slipped away from the sidelines and climbed into the bus parked at the curb. He sat in the back doing some calculus homework, peaceful and content behind the green-tinted window. His coach came in and asked him if he wanted to go out again.

"We can get you in," he said. "It's not too late."

"No, I'm all right." He waited out the game. He heard the boos and the cheers – the boos for a near fight in the end zone when San Marino scored yet again, and the cheers for the TDs that kept coming – until the boys from Bell Gardens filed in, beaten real good but taking heart in Harold's hit.

They talked it up on the way home. "He leveled his stupid ass, and the rest of them felt it. Pig fuckers, cornholers," the Okies said. Rank epithets once reserved for the Mexicans got thrown at the San Marino princes now, the real enemy.

"Rich bastards."

"Sons of thieving bitches."

The San Marino coach almost brought it up again at the league meeting, phoning his reaction to the Bell Gardens coach, furious and judgmental, but hearing another version from him. "Watch the game film if you want, I don't give a fuck," he said. Coach Hernandez was a crazy Chicano from neighboring Pico Rivera who loved football and kids, with no strings attached, and hated bullshit. He told Harold how it had gone down.

"The fucking whistle hasn't blown yet, and if you don't believe me, ask your kids. On the other hand, don't ask those punks. They were talking trash all night, all of them, and he got what he deserved. You heard me? What he deserved!" Coach Hernandez screamed out a few of the racial epithets that had been used against everybody. Even the Okies heard their share. "We'll go all the way with this if you want to, man. But I wouldn't. I'll make a stink about it all the way up to the state board, the CIF. I'll call the *LA Times* and it'll be a bigger story than you ever wanted. I don't give a fuck, Coach."

Crazy Lupe Hernandez.

"Get me fired, too, and meet me in the alley, pig fucker."

"Jesus, where do your kids learn this stuff, huh?"

"And yours?"

"*Señor* Hernandez?"

"Right."

It wasn't worth the risk of not coming out on top, of not smelling rosy – San Marino next door to old Pasadena and its guarded aristocracy, what passed for breeding then in Southern California – of not preserving that image so carefully tended of well-mannered, fine young men in the better parts of our city.

The coach from San Marino dropped it. Harold joined the team the next week and went on that famous late season tear that got him in the newspapers, all right, even the *Times*, but for the right reasons. He dominated the fields of Southern California on the losing run of his team, managing to balance out the losses with the honors he received, All-League, All-City, All-County, All-American. He had a lot of fun doing what he did best his last year, creating mayhem on the field, causing hurt and bruises in the approved way, and when I saw him between games, he laughed with me, catching me up on the latest with him.

"Fucking Frank, man. Where you been? How come you don't hang around with us no more?"

"I do, man, you just never see me. I'm a ghost – here, there, and everywhere."

Harold, ambitious Harold, applied to the many colleges that showed an interest in him – the colored brochures highlighting the pristine campuses fairly filling his mailbox, he said, and the calls from the coaches keeping him busy, most of them representing small schools. (He wasn't that big himself, a mere 5'10" or so, but a giant among Chicanos, and strong, bench-pressing a stack of 45-pound weights on either end of the bar that still stands as a record at Bell Gardens High, and mean and quick and cruel and smart on the field, a prime player.) He sent back the forms, extolling his own virtues ("Cub Scouts to Webelos, man, I put it in there!"), and wished himself luck getting in.

He thought his chances were pretty good at all of them, but the main one, the one he had his eye on, accepted him. The Air Force Academy at Colorado Springs sent him the treasured fat envelope. The boyhood interest in jets – model airplanes hanging from every corner of his room – culminated in his entry into the ranks of the flying gladiators. Harold, All-American, fighting ace and preserver of American soil ...

It took me by surprise but didn't shock me. I chuckled with him, watching him turn serene when I asked him why he wanted to leave Los for an academy in the boonies.

"I hear it's nice up there, close to the mountains."

"You're going to be a fighter pilot, right?"

"I don't know – I guess. I want to get up there, anyway," he rubbed his chin and fell into his Chicano routine, the one that cracked us up more and more now.

"Check out the view from above."

I laughed long and hard with him. Then I got serious, thinking about the possibilities that lay before him.

"Fuck the mountains. Fly the jets."

"From the dreamer himself," he said. "When are you taking off?"

"I don't know, man, as soon as I get my transcripts sent, all that stuff."

"All right, man, where you going?"

"As far away as I can, Harold. I want out."

"Why?"

"I don't know, lots of things. Fucking Harold," I pushed his shoulder a little bit, "Von Harold, de la chingada, Dutchman, German, what the fuck are you?"

"Mexican." He paused and stared hard at me. "American." Then he broke into his routine again, and shook his head, "De la chingada."

I saw a jet soar over Fresno the other night and thought of him, all those Chicanos going to the Persian Gulf, confused motherfuckers, All-American motherfuckers, hardcore, gangbanging, cholo motherfuckers, proud Mexican-American motherfuckers, puro Chicano y nada más motherfuckers, Americans of Mexican descent motherfuckers, crazy motherfuckers all, each and every one of them carrying a little locura deep inside, heading to the war in the sands. And Harold, does he wish he were going there, too? If he hadn't bombed out of the Air Force Academy at Colorado Springs, would he like to be streaking across the sky on his way to a glorious mission? Piloting an F-15 over Baghad?

I think he would, but then again, I'm not sure. He discovered the mountains when he was out there, and spent most of his time hiking. That newfound love contributed to his downfall. His reluctance to *buckle up,* in the words of his Commander, *and bite the bullet,* was aggravated by his desire to get up there, on those peaks, and climb. He admitted to me later that he was already getting tired of the whole military on his second day there, when they had them shining shoes and all that shit. "About-facing until I'd had about enough of it."

The planes didn't look so grand, either, after a while; they were just planes. He let the English slide.

I think he could've done it.

Or maybe not.

He couldn't write an essay worth shit and laughed about it with me, the struggling writer, expressing stupefaction when I told him I couldn't write either.

"Worth shit!" And we laughed again, toasting our failures.

What else is there to do?

So he bombed out, and came back to LA.

He was down for a while. He was up before you knew it. He told his parents he didn't want to work. Demanding, severe people with their kids, they wanted the best for them.

That's all, they said, the best. But they'd have to pay for it, in America, con ganas, con trabajo, with all those Mexican virtues they believed in translated into American terms. Con dee-sire, they'd say, emphasizing the d, dee-sire.

"Why do you think we moved here? Got you out of East LA, that hellhole?" they'd start off, in Spanish. "Dee-sire. To get better," they'd end, in English.

And Harold would flip a towel over his back and walk out the door. "I'm going out, I'm going to the mountains. I'm going swimming. Déjame en paz." Never looking back when they followed him outside and saw that he meant it as he got into their car, without asking, to go to the San Bernardino mountains, his refuge, to relax: laze around the boulders and look at the water streaming into more water. "It was bad, Frank," he said, lapsing into his old Chicanese, our old Chicanese, our real language. "I just did nothing for a couple of weeks."

"Yeah?"

"Yeah."

"Shit, man, I've been doing that all my life."

"Don't lie. You're always involved with something, motherfucker, making your plans. College. You're not doing nothing."

"You're right, Harold, I'm not. How's Rosa? I heard you guys are an item again! Out on the town like old times!"

"En el barrio," he let it out, and we both started laughing at the turn in his life, back in Rosa's arms, hanging out with her at the hot spots in Commerce, Rosa draped over him casually, with a predictable look on her face, *he's mine*, enlivened by a sparkle in her eyes that kept him up.

"I'm in love. Enamorado, ése, like a sad fish on the grill of life."

"Shut up, Harold. Don't try to write on your feet, ése. Dudes have been shot for less."

"Fucking Frank."

"Fucking Harold."

She came into his life again; they made it easily, simply, work. And more than deciding this was a good thing for both of them, the new start and the high hopes and the putting away all that was sordid and immature in the past, plus apologizing for the panty bet, a sore point between them, it signaled a deeper change in him.

It brought out the best in him. But the panty bet had gotten her mad, ferociously mad, because it came with details we demanded of Harold after a few beers in the pizza parlor – "C'mon, Harold, fucker, cough it up, the whole story. Tell us how you get down with a queen and what it feels like," and Harold, with a sly grin, told us all that happened, reaching into some perverted strata of human existence that I hope, myself, never to hear of again – details that reached her through the soggy grapevine of Commerce's hot news.

"Did you say that about me? Asshole? Pretend it was me?"

"No. Yeah. What the fuck's the difference?"

"I'm the difference, idiota! What were you thinking?"

"I wasn't."

"Right. You weren't."

They met at the bar and hung out, courted at the pub we called our own, as if the sign outside – Maggie's Pub – welcomed more than the locals who bellied up to the bar but loved them less. As if it was our neighborhood pub shut off from the world at large, even though it stood on teeming Washington Boulevard, drawing in the after-work blue-collar crowd and the office set and the red-faced executives for the healthy drinks and darts.

"This is all right, ha? Yeah?"

"Yeah, dude, the best."

Harold recognized her, did a double take, washed his face in the bathroom, combed his hair, and came out with a bright smile: *I'm here, your mate.*

He looked stupid for a while, got his bearings, tripped all over himself again when he realized maybe, just maybe, she'd take him; he wasn't such a bad guy after all. He fell in love.

He started soaring again. He was always wanting to take off, anyway, and it was a good thing watching him become himself, become more than himself. Love. What can I say about that? *Love.* Harold, up in the sky at last ...

"Here we go, into the wild blue yonder," we sang, gently, in the right spirit, neither mockingly nor too sweetly, when we met for a round at the pub. It was with less and less frequency, the old gang getting together, the dudes coming home from college or the military to sit in front of big pitchers of beer, on vacation, on leave, hell, one of us on the lam.

And Harold in his element, flying high, beaming, wise, spectacular.

"Harold, man, snap out of it."

"Okay, fucker, I'll snap out of it, all right. Waitress! Another pitcher, please! And clean the drool off this guy's face! He's embarrassing me!"

"Goddamn you, Harold. Get a grip, man."

"Grip what? I got your grip ..."

And then we looked up and Rosa had stopped by. She put us on notice. She was one of those gorgeous women for whom you wish to remember all that your mother ever taught you. You pulled out the chair for her and cleared your throat and hoped for the best with Harold, that fucker, and the rest of the slobs around you. You didn't want to be the fool anymore.

Rosa Pimental. Rosa Pimental. Nuestra reina de Commerce. Our queen of the barrio streets that weren't *barrio* at all: neighborhood goddess.

She took a seat among us. A vestige of Mexican formality directed our actions, and it was nice. I liked it, being courteous and decent and kind. Being nice.

It had been years since we had been so nice. It made me think, sometimes, of that night. Shamefacedly, I would hang my head and stare into my beer and think about it all. It was pretty chickenshit, pretty awful, really; we should never have done that. We clipped his wings before the Air Force ever did. That's for sure.

"I just wanted a drink."

"I'll get it, what kind?" Harold said.

"Relax, Harold. She likes you."

Then Harold eased up, and added, staring into his beer, which I taught them to drink, the ol' Berkeley twist, by the gallons, "Don't start, fucker, don't start."

"Okay, I'm not. I'm going home."

"No, pull up a chair and shut up."

"Okay. Sorry, Rosa. Did I do that?"

"It's all right. It's only a fingernail."

"Rosa, I'll buy you a new one!" Changes in taste, too, separated us, inevitably. Impoliteness on my part made me feel bad. But it didn't even register. I hadn't offended.

"It's okay, Frankie. You're too wound up."

I edged out of the story, sat at the outermost side of the table and drank, got lost in my own dreams and desires, which were big, too big maybe, but they kept me going. It was my style, and I wasn't going to give it up for anybody, until I had to.

And sometimes, sitting there in the pub, not even drunk but staring abstractedly, I would see Harold turn into a cholo before my eyes. I would blink hard and look away, fast, adjusting the heel of my shoe, maybe, to refocus and concentrate on something else. Just get the hell out of my thoughts. Go back to the good brown beer and lie.

We were all ethnic, different, separate. We were stamped alien against everybody else in America. And that's a lie, too, a big lie. I drank more beer, as usual. The music got louder. Standing on the table, I performed a Mexican polka but stayed rooted in my chair, thinking. I became a cholo knifing a rival in an alley but went nowhere, thinking. I became a doctor walking across a college stage with a sarape thrown over my shoulder but only took in the lights, thinking. I became a fucked up writer with flashes of brilliance but cleared my throat and called for another round, thinking. I became the one hundred and one possibilities of being a Chicano in America and left out one, too, whatever it is, still waiting …

We roughed up Harold pretty bad that night. We fucked him up but good.

We let him play his game. He led us around into what we called the jungle, the dark part of the park. And then when he thought he had us cowed, we reacted. We started small, "Hey, what's this shit, man?" and then advanced on him, "Fucking cholo, stupid ass" whistling through our teeth like some bad shit was going to come now. Watch out.

A scared dude asked, "What should we do, man?" and when as one everybody gave me the eye, asking me what to do, seeking in me some response to Harold freaking out under the brim of his black fedora with the red feather, his eyes shifting and bright, I knocked the hat off his head and pushed him.

He started to say my name, "Fra—," but I didn't even let him finish.

I yelled, "Kick his ass, kick his fucking ass!" and drove the first punch in.

We left him there on the ground, a mess below, getting some last kicks in and making him cover his face. A scary gasp from him caused us to stop. We were all breathing hard, and clenching our fists and swearing. "Motherfucker, get up then." When he staggered off, we followed him, pushing him around but not so bad anymore, and slapping his head.

He wouldn't turn on us because we'd kill him; we'd beat his ass so fucking bad he'd never get up again. He made it to the park bench where he sat down facing the basketball courts. They were empty and dark, dead tonight except for our shallow breaths sending up plumes of cold. It was bright and crisp.

After a while he stood up. He didn't say anything, not even a thank you for our attention. Ha! He just gathered himself, rising from the bench with deliberation, as if he knew we wouldn't fuck with him now – and we wouldn't; he was another guy already, another kid we'd like to get to know – and shot us through with one defiant glance before taking off across the field again, hat in hand, only crushed now, and pants dirty, shirt soiled with his own blood, shoes ruined, and body bruised.

Soul unscathed. Ha! Ain't I a joker?

He acknowledged the TJs on the sidelines, gave them a sharp salute walking past them under the slanting rays of the field lights. Then Harold the cholo drifted out of sight.

He burned his clothes or donated them to charity in East LA. Folded them up and sent them away. Even his chingón khakis. Maybe they still walk in the meanest projects de Los, covering the scarred legs of a vato needing them more than Harold ever did, simón.

When he made the football team the next year he came into his own. He fit in suddenly and impressed the girls, the guys, everybody. Brought home some all-league honors and earned a snapshot in the local paper, with a nice paragraph under it: "Harold Lopez: Local Star Shines."

The rest of his school years went as well, his years there in Commerce and at Bell Gardens High, bused in every day until he took the faux low-rider his senior year, the one his parents almost let him cherry, and spun us around for good times on Friday nights – the locals, his buddies, the half dozen or so friends he could count on – Harold, the gilded chauffeur.

We got drunk together and shared dark secrets, there on the railroad tracks near where we first discussed Bell Gardens and Okies and Catholic school and my charming ways with the girls. Ha! And confessed the worst of our sinful selves in blubbering sessions, these same guys who hung pretty tightly in those days, no matter what, smoking pot now and fucking and fucking up, too, again and again.

We kidded around and managed. But when we spoke of certain things it was still in hushed tones, as if we didn't quite trust each other not to burst the dams inside us and make us cry for real, in a way that nobody wanted anybody else to see.

We knew what was taboo. We knew when to shut up.

We never talked about it again. It touched something so deep and personal in him that we backed off, knowing that to bring it up would be to risk real violence now, like bringing up some awful family secret you wanted hidden away forever. Like bringing up the fact of my sick father easing the pain with a bottle at his side. Like dwelling on that for kicks.

We didn't say any more. We had done our duty by him and the rest was history. Harry, All-American, más loco que la chingada, eh?

We turned him around in our direction. We manhandled him for going the route of a killer, a kingly vato, a leading player on those streets. It was just Harold, good old Harold himself, former Cub Scout chum and Catholic school nerd we wanted. We wanted a regular guy, an all-right guy, like me, like all the rest forming our group.

And we got him. We got Harold, All-American, our friend, regular guy and all-around hero, in our neighborhood.

CHATO'S DAY

"I can't hang anymore, honey," Chato sputtered into the pre-paid cell phone he had stolen a few days ago, pocketing it quickly at Thrifty's.

Now he was standing in an abandoned phone booth outside a liquor store. Cars were passing up and down the street as he talked, but Chato, hanging his head low, shouted over them. He put his finger in his ear and waited. Chato, feeling out of place in a neighborhood that wasn't his, let out a long, slow breath. It was so simple, man, simple. He waited for a response, dangling the keys in his pocket while he looked up at the sky through the green-colored glass scratched with graffiti: "Honey, do you hear me?"

"Yeah, I hear you. Wait a minute, okay?" She didn't say anything else, but then, quietly, on the other end, it came through: "It's Chato, he's drunk."

"Okay, hang up."

"No, I can't just hang up. Like that." She made him wait again, and then returned, as if she was irritated with him and in a hurry. "Okay, Chato, what d'you want?"

"I want you, baby, I love you." Chato could picture her so fine in tight black stretch pants and a glittery blouse with her name or something splashed across the front: *Sophisticated Lady*.

"It's over, Chato, I already told you that."

"Okay, babe, if that's the way you want it."

"That's not the way I want it, Chato, you know that." Her voice stopped again, and Vera leaned against the wall in her kitchen, studying her fingernails. Chato knew her habits better than she did.

Her fingernails shone black, with bursts of silver. Her sister did them for her.

She was a young chick still with more sense than Vera, who was doing everything to please her. She wanted her to go away. She got on the line again.

"Chato, come see me then."

"Okay, babe, I'm on my way."

Chato hopped on the bus pulling up at the curb and sat in the back by an old lady snoozing over a bag. When he got off at the corner near Vera's, he made sure to fix up his hair in the window of a furniture store before he headed down her block. He had a trim mustache, neat but with a small harelip notching it, wore a dark sweatshirt and light brown pants that folded high on his black suede slip-ons, like mini accordions or something. He kicked out his legs to straighten them, then relaxed and forgot about it. He was on his way to see Vera and what the fuck did he care about pants now?

Except maybe getting out of his and into hers! Órale. He still had his sense of humor after a day like today, so maybe he was going to be all right after all. He got a move on.

Here we go, big guy, let's do it. Chato was strolling down the street kind of bowlegged and proud. On his arms the heavy duty statement he had considered and reconsidered before getting it inked bulged below the short sleeves of his sweatshirt – *Chicano Power* – and rose and fell on each triceps in heavy Gothic script, *Chicano* on the left, *Power* on the right. In between, above a muscular back veeing up to the pretty big shoulders, the tat on his neck spelled it out: *FRESNO*.

He was from the Big Fresno – 27 and full of fire – even though no one from his neighborhood liked him because he was too crazy, so they said. He liked to fight when people called him stupid – what was crazy about that? – and stabbed a guy not too long ago but tried not to think about it much. The vato deserved it and it was a sad story he wished he didn't have a part in.

His two babes watched over him, anyway. They stayed with him, peeking out from behind the words stretching down his triceps and winking long eyelashes at anybody checking him out, a pair of fine Chicanas under detailed sombreros flipped up at the brims with his name drawn in, *Chato* on one, *Montoya* on the other. Emilia and Pancha he named them. They pouted so hot he could barely keep himself from spinning around to see them, lifting up his arm and catching a glimpse over his shoulder.

Again. Bad girls, naughty girls, Chato's kind. Except for Vera. She was one of a kind. Both bad and good and something in between, but mostly herself, which kept him coming back.

The last touch had been her name in the same Gothic lettering where nobody could see it. It ran down his side from his armpit to his waist, with a serpent in green slithering through the letters and sticking out its tongue at the V, which was in the shape of a woman's legs, spreading.

"Goddamn you," she had laughed when she saw it. "You're fucking crazy!"

"Yeah, I am," he said, "for you."

He never tried to hide it. He was in love with Vera.

"All Gothic, ése," a huilo junkie had told him in the County. "Put on more and paint yourself green. You'll be like Frankenstein waking up." The dude imitated the sewn-up monster staggering out of the place on the hill.

"I wouldn't mind, ése. With a bride like that who could complain?" Electrified eyes belonging to the bride of Frankenstein had brought up an image of Vera licking his balls in a charged honeymoon they blew out the walls with, and he had laughed.

"And the castle's free." He had gotten too deep for the dude, he thought, even surprised himself with that one.

"Ah, what is it with this Gothic shit," Chato had said. "It's just fucking lettering. I like it. If it was called Chicano I'd probably get more."

"Simón." The dude wanted to move away from the conversation now. "Chicano is cool."

Chato reached her house. It was a mildewed two-bedroom with cobwebs hanging from the windows that he knocked down with a broom sometimes. An old glider on rusted chains filled up half the porch next to the front door, with stuffing coming out of the cushions in bunches.

They had swung on it a few times and held hands, when they first met.

"What are your dreams, Chato?"

"You."

"What about me?"

"Getting you in bed and making you mine."

"Ay, Chato, that's all you think of, ha?"

"Yeah. That and fixing this piece of shit slider, glider, whatever you call it. It squeaks so much I'm gonna go crazy trying to get it out of my head. Eek eek eek." He made the sound of a mouse. "Like a mouse or something. It's driving me nuts."

"You already are, Chato, man."

"I know it, man, for you."

"Buy me a big fucking ring."

"Can I put it down there and stick my tongue in it?"

"Chato!"

Those had been good days for them. They had spent a lot of time just fooling around and laughing at the bad made-up jokes he threw at her, and fucking. When they did it, Chato forgot about everything. All his worries drifted away. But it had been a long time since they had made love.

He sprang up on her porch and tried her doorbell, hearing the shrill ring in his ears before he realized it didn't work. *Dead dead dead* ran like a current through his mind. Then he pounded twice, hard, with the heel of his hand. *Pam! Pam!*

"C'mon, man, Vera, where are you?" A little desperation crept into his voice but he didn't speak up clearly. He talked to himself like he always did, practically mumbling.

This afternoon at the fucking job site, the gabacho had asked him, "What can you do?" friendly enough, not really mean, and Chato, who couldn't do shit but felt he could do everything for that kind of job – basic construction with lots of muscle required and no skills, only the few he had already picked up from here and there – dropped his eyes again and mumbled something about experience and know-how.

"What?" The gabacho had pressed him, and Chato had gotten pissed, raising his head and blurting out, "I'll do whatever the fuck you want me to, man."

Then he had given a little speech that he was even proud of. He didn't know where the words came from. They just poured out of him as he stared the boss straight in his blue eyes that didn't quiver or blink but almost clouded up with concern as he squinted and studied him: "I'll clean your fucking toilets. I'll pound your nails. I'll carry your shit. I'll do the worst work for the lowest fucking pay because I'm a fucking Mexican." There, he had given the boss a reason not to hire him, and he wouldn't now. He was sure of that.

But the gabacho had only backed off a step, observing him, not hating him yet.

"Okay." The big freckled dude had filed his application in a folder with others. "We'll call you when we need you. Phone number is correct, right?"

Chato held the stolen prepaid cell phone up to his ear. "You can get me anytime, man, here and at the other number I left you, at the house."

"Right, right, thanks."

So that's the way the afternoon had gone, and now he was here at Vera's. He was standing on her porch looking down at his worn-out slip-ons. He pointed them up at himself and heard them talking: "Chato, the biggest fool in town, you're an asshole, waiting here on this porch for this bitch you love. Eres menso, ése, menso." The soles wagged at him like tongues going mad with his own words. Words that he fed them, himself. Why was he doing that? He wasn't that stupid.

He couldn't blame it on the beer, either. It was hardly anything. Like only a six-pack he had gulped when he ran into some dudes he knew from the County, drinking in a garage. They got him buzzed. They got him feeling good. That's all.

"Where you going, ey?" a slim vato in the garage had asked him when he got up to leave.

They were all sitting around a picnic table as if they were kicking back at the park, not inside a garage under the broken lights above. A rotted rigging of fluorescent tubes rusted in the ceiling. Thin wires suspended it on either end. He began to get freaked out because he imagined Frankenstein getting up from his table, looking around, and asking for Vera.

He was hooked up to the main voltage through the wires attached to bolts in his head, and the switch-thrower was God standing behind the curtain of an old snapshot booth gathering dust in the corner of the garage, hiding like the Wizard of Oz.

"Where'd you get that, ey?" he asked.

"My old man. He brings home all kinds of shit from the swap meet and never does shit with it. It just stays here. Want it?"

"Naw, I'll probably just take my picture all day mugging for the camera like a con. I ain't no fucking con."

"What's your trip, ey? Nobody said you were a con."

"Naw, but I seen you guys looking at me like I'm a freak or something. The beer was fine, ey. But not in this company."

"Check him out."

"Check who out? I'm going to see my old lady, ey. Anybody stands in my way, I'm taking him down."

They were getting up from the table in the tight garage, with Chato standing bowlegged at the head of the table, a last beer in his hand, eyeing them as he gulped it.

"Are those fair rules, or what?" He laughed and stepped outside into the sunlight. He stood in the driveway now.

"You guys are fucked up, ey. Inviting me over for beer and then talking about my old lady that way."

He waited for them to say something. But they didn't. They just stood there looking at him.

"See, you want to know everything."

"He's crazy, ey," the dude he knew better said to the other two. They stood in the shadows of the garage still. They looked more confused than scared or ready to spring.

"You know what, I'm getting the fuck out of here," Chato said, realizing he had done nothing wrong in this exchange except everything. They hadn't done anything bad.

"You guys are all right, ey, I'm just a little fucked up," he pointed upstairs, "in the head."

"All right, ey, don't come back until you're better." The host of the little party already turned his back on him.

"I ain't got time for this shit either."

"And somebody's gonna get hurt," the güero with the goatee said, almost loud enough for Chato to have to fire back but not quite, "gonna get hurt real bad for some silly shit that ain't worth it."

They went back to sitting at the table with fresh beers in their hands.

They had pulled them out of the refrigerator, the only working machine in the place.

"All right, ey, all right," he mumbled to himself walking down the street.

He stepped into the phone booth outside the liquor store, called Vera, and made his way over, already sobering up. He hurried down to her pad. He could drink okay, not the hard stuff but beer, drink it like water, and pump iron and carve his name in the wall at home if he wanted to. When he was bored, *Chato con Vera* came out like a teenager's declaration on the cheap plaster in his bedroom.

He turned the blade on his arm at night, slowly bringing out a thin line of blood with a bead at the end to prove that he was human, not a monster, the way he felt with his fucking harelip and short temper. He couldn't even get along with people who wanted to help him, not hurt him, just party down with him and shit like that. He'd get mad just at the sound of their voices, their stupid fucking voices. Everybody had a life but him.

"Get a job, Chato, or hit the road," she had said, not too long ago. She had brought on their problems. Not hers, exactly, but his.

"Hers, too, man," he thought. "She still answers the phone when I call. What the fuck is she thinking if she doesn't love me anymore?" Chato used the L word in connection with Vera because she had spit it into his ears enough times to leave no doubt about her feelings.

They made crazy fucking passionate love, Chato pulling her panties down with one swift hand, giving her no time to resist, and, spreading her legs fast with the other, using his strength if he had to, but never really needing it because her stunned look always invited him in. When he slipped inside her, it was like falling in space, flying in the middle of the stars and white creamy stuff filling the Milky Way, with Carl Sagan standing off to the side talking about "billions and billions" of little Chatos forming for a second and smiling happily in all the blackness that made up the universe when he finally made her come and exploded himself.

She yelped happily. He lay on top of her breathing hard, and she clutched at his ears, at his head, and whispered, "I love you, Chato, don't believe me when I'm such a bitch. I don't know what the fuck I want either. But I want you in the game, ése, if you can get your shit together."

"Billions and billions …"

"What?"

"That dude Carl Sagan always makes a guest appearance in my head when I make love to you."

"That's fucking weird, Chato. Get the fuck out of here."

"Okay, baby, I'm leaving."

That's the way their last lovemaking ended, and he couldn't even remember when that was. He had even seen her out with another dude once, crossing the street to get into a car as he turned the corner on her block with a bouquet of flowers he stole from Safeway.

He didn't really steal so much, but sometimes he needed things and was in a hurry. At least he was never in the County for anything serious like murder or strong-armed robbery or dealing heroin. Just the regular small stuff sent him to the bench behind the bars, waiting and waiting to finish up his sentence and get on with his life again.

"My life, man, where is it?" he thought on the porch, eyeing the houses he knew by heart in this part of Fresno, not too far from his own, knew from standing out here just like this. It was near the railroad tracks where things held their own, barely. Rundown duplexes and tinier frame houses stood behind patches of browning lawn and sagging fences.

Hers was okay, not the best, not the worst.

"Vera, get your ass out here," he muttered glumly, and pounded on the door again, this time kicking the bottom before Vera answered in a sheer nightgown piped with black and teased hair going up all old-school, slitting her eyes.

"Chato, man, I'm so fucking horny I want you to fuck me all day the way you want to fuck me. Make me yours, Chato, make me yours." She reached out and pulled him in through the door.

"Fat fucking chance," he thought, "I'm a maníaco and she's a frigid bitch now."

When he saw her getting into the car, he smashed the flowers against the curb and ran home. He sat on the crate in the garage he spent a lot of time in because his mother had too many "visitors" for him to handle.

His old lady always pissed him off with her loose ways around men, set him off bad. She started when his father died and left them both alone, so many years ago he didn't even know when. He didn't even know how anymore. He was just a little boy with a hole in his life. When she first brought men over, he took off outside, sat on the steps for a while or just went roaming the streets and ended up at the park sometimes where he learned how to fight and play caroms until he got older and turned to pool.

"Harelip."

"Your mother's lips." He threw blows so good he became known. Pretty soon everybody left him alone, and he walked in a bubble separating him from the world.

He sometimes spent the night on the streets, just walking. He knew she loved whoever she was staying with that night more than him.

Chato was pissed off still, but he didn't want to do anything stupid with anybody, like cut him. He had cut that one dude out of fear at a card game when he sensed that he was already ripping him off and wanted more, all that he had, in a setup the other dudes were kind of in on. He had sprung up and struck fast, upwardly and forcefully, sticking him good until they pulled him off and saved the cheating motherfucker.

Enough dudes in the room knew how to apply a butterfly bandage to a cut like that and keep him alive until the ambulance came. "Fucking Chato, man, what'd you do?"

"Almost killed this fucker for almost stealing my money. What do you think?"

The dude was gurgling on his back and holding his side but hardly looking at Chato, more at the clock on the wall.

"Let me finish it and I'll save us both the trouble."

"Get the fuck out of here, Chato. You're cool with the cops. But get the fuck out of here."

"All right, I'm out of here. But I don't give a shit if he dies or not."

The next night he had done something almost as stupid as the night before. He had stepped up on the crate in the middle of the garage, throwing a rope over a beam, and tied a good strong knot that he stuck his head in and checked for strength. It wasn't perfect but just fine for what he planned to do: step off and swing into the future, hands clasped behind his back like a cuffed vato without appeal. Just swing, baby, swing.

He had stepped down when the light, funneling out from a yellow bulb in the ceiling, cast a shadow three times bigger than him on the garage wall. "Shit, man, that's me," he said, with the noose around his neck and his shoulders hunched up to his ears in fear and excitement. Fuck it, he was ready for the big swing.

But then he started trembling and shaking. He didn't want to be remembered that way. He didn't want to kill himself when he could, instead, do something good like give somebody else life.

"And I'm still hanging from there," he reminded himself on the porch. "I got to get down from there, for good."

The door opened. "C'mon in, Chato. What took you so long?" Turning like a queen in the small hall that led to the living room that was usually picked up but not today, Vera wore a black fringe shawl around her barely covered shoulders and tight, tight Levi's with black high heels and a shiny belt to match. Her lipstick glistened black, and heavy blue eye shadow made up her eyes. She was beautiful.

"You look good with a rope around your neck," he said, and reached out and squeezed her neck until her eyes popped out.

"Chato," she gasped out the name and cried. "You're fucking crazy!"

"I am," he dropped his hands and shook his head, "not. But I finally got my shit together, baby." He spoke clearly, meeting her eyes when she blinked away her fears.

He wasn't going to kill her after all. "This morning, I got a job. Right after I talked to you."

"No, you don't," she backed off into the living room, stroking her neck. "You're not coming in here, ey. Get the fuck out of here."

"Yes, I am, baby," he said. He followed her in anyway. She spun around nervously, confused by his intensity, he could tell, throwing pillows out of the way and plopping herself down on the couch.

"Sit here, Chato, and tell me about it. Don't be so fucking weird." She was massaging her neck still. "You almost fucking killed me, ey. What was that about? I oughta call the cops on you."

"I just shook you a little bit. Don't lie. You know I love you enough to care."

"You're fucking crazy, ey. What's this about a job?"

But Chato only grinned. He sat next to her on the long couch with his hand creeping towards hers, feeling the pleasant tingle of the electricity buzzing through his body that must have been from the phone ringing in his pocket.

"It's a miracle, ésa. I'm alive."

LA GLORIA MEETS LA HELEN
EN LA MARQUETA AND WHAT IS
BEST LEFT UNSAID IS FOR YOU

para mi nieta
y todos who might read this in the future and whenever

Hey, Helen, what are you doing?"

"Pues nada, ésa, just hanging around." Like that's what she was doing that day, just hanging around, looking a little lost and confused in the marqueta.

She didn't look too good. Especially around the eyes she looked a little sad.

I reached for her arm, but not too much.

"You sure, ésa, you okay?" I said, barely touching her.

"Yeah, I'm okay, Gloria," she said. "I ain't bad at all."

She looked at me, kind of smiled and mumbled.

Then I let her go.

Because all kinds of people were already looking at us. Always you get two cholas together talking the old talk you get like stares, putdowns from old times, way back, coming up around you.

So I let her go. She just walked down the aisle by herself.

She didn't look too good that day. She looked real skaggy as a matter of fact.

She wore one of those old leather miniskirts, black and faded. Hers looked worse because it had like half the nalgas worn out with shine and the other half buffed to a mellow black.

I'm a poet, ha?

Or maybe it was the other way around come to think of it. Half the nalgas worn out with wear and the other shining brightly from who knows where.

Ha!

And she went dragging her ass down the aisle, la Helen did, just dragging it.

On a Saturday night I saw her. I was just in there for a few things myself.

It was such a change to see her.

From the old days she had come a long way, baby. Or not such a long way, baby, if you know what I mean.

If you get my drift you're on to what I'm trying to tell you. She had sunk real low with the years.

In the old days la Helen ruled us all. She was fine, firme, de aquellas. A broad that you can be proud of was la Helen when she led us, de veras.

And now she had sunk to this. A street girl, a hooker on the streets was la Helen again. A few times in the years past I had caught up to her.

Always the same old song with la Helen it was. Barely saying hello to each other we did when it was worse.

Then it got better sometimes. Then it got bad again.

For us all as a matter of fact you might say it got pretty bad. But it was better before that, for sure.

During those years I was on top of the world. With la Helen on the bottom I didn't pay her much mind.

Not that I had anything bad to say, you know, I didn't. But just staying on top of my own game, of my own life, if you know what I mean, was enough for me.

I gave her all I could whenever I saw her hurting so, so … veterana.

"Helen, how you doing?" I'd say, grabbing her arm in the marqueta. Or maybe it was outside the church where I'd see her once in a while. All bundled up in a sweater she'd be. She'd be like shivering even though it was June.

She'd be on the stuff then, too. All year she'd be shooting up, walking the streets, starting up in some program down south, then back on the streets again she'd be for a little while.

La Helen. She wasn't so bad then for a couple of months, a couple of years, tú sabes. Then down again.

But I gave her all I could while I could. Once I even gave her a ride.

So we were carnalas from way back.

La Helen and I go back to the old days in Fresno. When we were young it was bad.

And now I'm an old faded chola telling my tale. In the bad low-class way I talk I remind myself of me back then because you wouldn't believe who I am now.

A secretary.

I'm a secretary for a big-shot attorney in the city hall in the downtown of Fresno where the gabachos and the Mexicans all clean-cut and cute enter the halls of justice.

Ha!

I saw her sitting here a few times in my flush days.

And I went up to her and put an arm around her right in the middle of everybody. Sitting down next to her I scooted up to her real tight-like and whispered, "I love you, Helen," in her ear. "You're gonna make it."

But she was too far gone then to do anything for herself.

In and out of rehab she's been all these years. Sometimes crazy on the streets she's been.

That's after she was crazy with us. A different kind of crazy I'm talking about here.

When we were young it was fun and dumb. Now it's all serious and shit.

La Helen comes into my life again on a Saturday night and my life ain't so hot, neither. I'm divorced. The viejo left. He found himself another chick. What more can I say?

She was good-looking?

Yeah.

She was young?

Yeah.

He's an asshole from way back and I'm better off without two?

Yeah. No. I don't know, man.

Only that my life ain't so hot I know for sure now. Things are different than they were in the old days, I'll tell you that for sure.

Back in the old days we had fun, no matter what. We went out and partied. We fucked. We gangbanged.

Might as well admit some of the crazy shit I've done in my life, de veras, ése, Man above, God, I know you're up there. I've stabbed a chick high in an alley. I've beaten another one near to death. I've knocked an old lady over for her purse.

I've done all kinds of crazy shit, man, just to pass the time and have fun and be real. Be real is what I can't do no more.

It's what I find it hard to do now. I can't smile like in the old days.

They called me la Smiley, but let's not get into that because that's just gonna bring a lot of pain and heartache anyway. And those are two things I don't need right now, de veras. I got enough on my mind without more.

But I saw Helen the other day in the marqueta and she kind of sobered me up if you know what I mean. She was lingering in the potato chip aisle looking kind of stupid.

Then I went up to her. "Helen," I said, "how you been?"

But she barely recognized me really. Pushing her hair back she looked at me for a long time. Then she managed, "Gloria?" Kind of with a crooked smile she had.

She looked like she was on the verge of tears. Then she didn't cry or not cry.

Her face just kind of changed, ésa. She looked real bad, real sad.

Standing there in the middle of the Safeway we must have been a sight to see. Two old cholas from way back greeting each other with a lot of pain between them.

To tell you the truth I left out half the story. I just couldn't tell it, ésa.

It was just too painful. What we been through and all ain't nice, ain't pretty, ain't for polite ears, you might say.

I took a little college on my way here.

To the marqueta I drove in my Suburu. A little blue one with a black vinyl top I own.

Says "Glory" on the license plate because I was lucky to get that. Just told the guy at the DMV, "I want that!"

And when he said yes, kind of smiling and nodding, I thought, "Qué chavalo," him in the DMV in his pressed shirt and nice slacks, a new kid, a new worker there. He's Mexican American, or Chicano if he's got any sense. Handing out the new forms, he's all smiles.

And then I go walking out into the night. I mean from Safeway.

Where I saw Helen that night was in the one on Blackstone here in the old hometown of Fresno. She just stood there for a while shaking in front of me like she was ready to crack up. Then her eyes softened.

Then I reached for her, and she went on her way up the aisle minding her own business.

La Helen was one fine broad in her day.

Maybe she'll be back one day. Who knows? I don't. And you don't.

Whoever you are reading this story maybe one of these days don't know.

All I want to say, man, is that I saw her, and for like a split second or something we recognized each other again, and the old times came flooding back on me, like in a rush, and I saw my carnala standing in front of me all torn up and hurting, and I wanted to do something, but I couldn't, because I still carried all that weight from the past, because we loved each other once, we did, de veras, in ways that ain't fit for this story, if you know what I mean, ways that only carnalas and homegirls know about, and I was just left standing there, you know, with nothing to say, no words to say, to my old friend Helen, my carnala, walking up the aisle away from me.

"Wait, Helen," I wanted to say, but that won't work. In the end I guess we're all alone anyway.

But sometimes I don't feel so alone neither.

I see homeboys and homegirls from the old times around town. I see them in the parking lots and the stores, buying things, talking, sometimes down and out, sometimes doing real good, too.

We stop and talk, me and the old crowd de aquella tiempo. We laugh and have a cigarette. We cross the street into a coffee shop and bullshit all day.

Sometimes five minutes is more like an hour. Sometimes an hour turns into a dawn in bed with somebody you don't know.

Because we've all changed so much over the years it's hard to keep in touch with who you are. But they're there in front of me, the old crowd, reminding me of who I was and who I am always.

They're there in front of me laughing and gabbing, putting on some big show for my sake always.

"Gloria! Long time no see!" And then some ruca's squealing into my arms, and then some vato's giving me a hug.

It's all right. These intimate little moments that happen are okay.

Say, last week I ran into somebody from the old crowd at the library. He was looking into some books on real estate, saying he was going to make a killing on the houses over on the west side of town, the fucked up side of town, selling them to wetbacks for way more than they're worth.

Then when I told him, "Sin vergüenza, man, leave them alone," he told me he was just jiving and didn't know what the fuck he was doing, either. Just checking out some books on this and that he was.

You see people like that around town, people you knew way back when, getting in touch with their roots. I mean they're not getting in touch with their roots.

They're just reading or something. Trying to make themselves better they are.

This is one way to do it. So you see some vato at the library once in a while checking out a book at the counter.

Or already at the door he is thumbing through his book on the way out. And then you spot each other and you go, "Hey, man, how's it going?" and you start talking for a while about this and that. Nothing special.

People come up, though. All these names from the shady past – ha, ha – float around us in the moment we enjoy each other's company.

Two sparkling eyes look at me. They are God's.

My life has been all right, man, not too bad. And if I wanted to admit the truth I could.

I fucked up. I fucked up real bad from way back.

And then I fucked up some more. But I cleaned up my act some, ésa, and when you see your granny walking down the street say with pride, "That's my abuela, ése, she did some good in her life, she was something."

Say it with pride. Don't turn away with shame from me, Ruby, who I'm writing this for after all.

You know more than me what you gotta do to survive. Be good, be strong, be mean and tough in the right ways.

Do what you want to do without hurting people, and when you do have to hurt people, do it with style. I don't know what I'm saying, Ruby. Forgive me.

She passed by me like a queen in the end. In the crazy aisles of that store I let her go by me.

La Helen, la ruca más loca de mi barrio Fresno, gathered herself up like a person worth remembering. And then she was out the door, Ruby, all fucked up into the night.

THE BARBERSHOP

y father walked up the sidewalk to Marcello's barbershop that day. He got going in a jerky gait that took him from the curb to the front door. He limped past the beauty shop next door on the busy street, and barely stopped at the entrance to wave goodbye to us.

We were sitting in the car watching him. We had just dropped him off.

Laboring, he measured each step, leaning on one side of his body, his left leg kind of dragging along the way it did. And he wore his dress-up clothes, dress-up for him, that is, who wasn't a fancy man but my father the working man taking on the sidewalk in good clothes.

He wore his corduroy jacket that looked kind of like a sports coat, more like a rancher's jacket, though, with a brown fur collar with leather lapels and big, thick buttons that were cracked on purpose. It was buttoned at the top and with his shiny work pants it looked kind of fancy, I guess, in the sunlight. Add to that his desert boots and his hair combed back slick.

He got in a fight with my brother in the house before we left.

"¿Qué estás haciendo?" he said, wild-eyed and upset that my brother moved towards him with the comb when my mom said he could go.

Sure, he could go to Marcello's for a haircut.

"Vamos al Marcello's," he had said, getting up from his place on the couch, and my brother and I looked around startled in the living room.

There were only the two of us watching TV with him, my mother and sister off in the yard hanging clothes, so we were the only witnesses.

"Did you hear that?"

"Yeah, I did."

"Dad, what'd you say?" It was astounding because my father hardly said anything anymore.

He just studied us with wandering eyes.

"Para cortar mi pelo," he said, and he made a ripping, anguished, gnawing motion with his hands, as if he were tearing his hair apart to demonstrate for us what he meant.

We knew what he meant. He wanted to get his hair cut at Marcello's barbershop.

We had gone to Marcello's a lot when we were kids. I mean kid kids – youngsters in booster seats licking lollipops after the big shave, head tilted down for Marcello's expert razor getting the neck hair, or standing around the punch bowl at Christmastime smelling the rum up, and then later, not too long ago, asking for special haircuts. I'm talking about going when things were all right, and we needed to get out of the house for escape and camaraderie, what you might call laughter among men.

Now we just sat around the house mostly, letting our hair get long and in our faces, making us feel awful. I felt awful, and my brother must have felt awful sitting there because he just got up, suddenly, looking pained.

He yelled, "Ma, Dad wants to go to Marcello's, to get his hair cut!"

And my mom popped in, dangling a wet blouse low to the ground and wiping her brow, asking us what we wanted again.

"A Marcello's, para cortar mi pelo," my dad managed to say, again with that anguished look as if it were costing him something to say every word, and he sat back down on the couch.

He had been leaning forward with that awful twist to his face.

Then my brother said, "Yeah, he wants to go to Marcello's."

"Para cortar mi pelo," my father mumbled.

He was that up.

My mom sighed, and said, "Okay, go," getting us out of the house for what would be my dad's last haircut there, but we weren't thinking that. We couldn't know it.

All we knew was we were going to the barbershop, Marcello's barbershop, like old times, maybe, but probably not, since my dad wasn't anything like in those days when Marcello would greet him with a big hand in the air, saying, "How's it going, Al? Take a seat!" And my father wouldn't let the day go by without saying something about the big shiny Cadillac parked behind the barbershop. "Man, one of these days, Marcello, I'll be driving one too."

"Sure you will, Al." He'd say something like this. "You probably got three already. For all those ladies you love." He'd say the last calmly, as if it were common knowledge that my father was the biggest playboy in town.

"Four, Marcello. Shiny, black, big."

"Aw, man, it's a dog's life," Marcello'd start in on the difficulty of everything after they'd had their laugh, and we'd wait our turn for a haircut sitting in the long airy room, facing the three brothers at work, Marcello, Henry, and Mariano – the Filipinos.

"C'mon, man, get a hold of him," my brother said. He was moving him towards the car.

He opened the door, holding my dad up by the waist, my dad groping for the handle, and I just stood back looking kind of important but really knowing I was useless. I reached forward to steady him in.

"There you go, Dad," I said.

My brother shot me a look to follow him to the other side, and I got in behind him. He started the car.

"Ready to go to the barbershop, Dad? Al Marcello's?"

"Sí, sí," my dad spoke up loud and clear.

He sat up straight as if readying himself for a big event. His hair was combed, slicked down and parted, and we had put on his best clothes capably, arranging him as if he were a set mannequin ready to come to life. He took stock of the walk ahead of him, paused for a moment on the sidewalk, and then started.

He made a tentative step towards Marcello's barbershop, limping on his bad leg, the leg he dragged more and more now. At home he used a cane stamped SANTE FE RAILROAD, practicing in the back yard for that day when he would get better. He never would, and he knew it, but he had to say something about why he bothered, walking up and down the drive-way on a sunny day in his undershirt and stained pants that were looser and looser on him, straight out of the dryer.

It was actually a broomstick cut in two, the cane, and embarrassed me. But right now I wasn't thinking of that at all.

He got a good rhythm going, as if he felt the cane under him without holding it, trudging forward on his bad leg with his good one catching up swiftly but recklessly, dangerously, and making it up to Pricilla's Beauty Shop next door to Marcello's barbershop – Commerce Barbershop – on the busy boulevard. He slowed in front of the door with the drawn venetian blinds – it was always closed, that place, never open – then headed straight for Marcello's.

We eyed him. "Get in there, Dad," my brother said, and we watched him disappear into the barbershop for the last time.

We went on our errands next. We just needed to kill some time before my father was done, and let him enjoy the barbershop, not just get a haircut. We didn't know that it was the last time or anything like that. We were just going with the day as best we could, as if it were a regular day for us, a normal day in our lives.

So we drove up Atlantic Boulevard to Pep Boys in East LA, and my brother picked up a bottle of Armor All and a chamois rag in aisle 7. My brother loved to wash and clean the car on weekends, spending a whole Saturday afternoon on the tires, whistling to himself and ignoring the mess inside for a little bit. He could forget that Dad was inside whimpering to himself in unceasing pain, rocking himself in slow, grieving motion.

"All right, man, he's in," my brother had said, and smiled at me, really one of the few times in a long time I had seen him smile that way, fully satisfied with what he had just seen.

So we edged into the busy street and rode past the familiar landmarks engraved in our heads because that's where we drove a lot with our father when he was well and we were together. Car lots and stuff like that on either side of the block created an avenue of misfortune and I almost started crying but didn't.

We were having a good day after all. We strode into Pep Boys like we were the biggest men on earth, taking time off from our busy schedules to give them some business. "Where you going, dude?"

"Aisle 7."

"All right. I'll be in the bike-stuff aisle near the sporting goods."

I liked that aisle a lot because it had everything that interested me in the store besides the occasional mini-bike that popped up in the corner, and I spent a little time checking out a mirror for my ten-speed. Then I moved on to the sporting goods hidden away at the far end of the aisle, feeling out the mitts in case I decided to get a new one this year and show them how it was done. I was a pretty good hitter and runner but not much of a fielder and I knew it, but I could pretend, scooping up grounders in the aisle like I was at Dodger Stadium playing in the World Series, saving a perfect game for Sandy Koufax.

"Okay, dude, let's go," my brother said, and I just wanted to stay there all day long, fantasizing about starring in a big game and not letting anybody down.

My brother walked up to me and put his hand on my shoulder because I was nearly sobbing, staring into the web of the glove now, just holding the damn thing in my hand, and he must have sensed it the moment he saw me.

"All right, man, let's get back to Dad, pick him up. He's having a good day."

"Did you pay for your stuff already?"

"Yeah, I did. Let's go."

I should have given my brother more credit than I did. He was an all-right guy with a lot of stuff on his mind and I guess I was unnecessarily harsh with my shitty kid-brother attitude those days, more like a smart teenager stuck in a little boy's body, always questioning his moves and attitudes when I didn't have to. He was pretty solid all around, taking care of my dad so much and doing his bit with the family budget, giving whatever he made in his current low-wage job to my mother. He was looking to go away to the Air Force as soon as all this was over.

"What'd you see, dude? Anything you want?"

"Naw, nothing, the usual, just some stuff in the bike aisle."

I broke it down for him on the way back. Then we stopped at a red light before going under the bridge that took us to Commerce and Marcello's barbershop, and he let out a big sigh as if he were depressed by what he saw.

The Tick-Tock Motel faced the street and it was pretty bad, with torn screen doors hanging open on dark caves where people lived, and couches outside holding a couple of derelicts. It wasn't a great place, and I was glad when the light changed and got us out of there.

"Let's go, man, get Dad," my brother said, reminding us of our mission. "He's probably all done now."

"Probably," I said, and stared at the graffiti on the walls going under the bridge.

So it would be better when we got there, I knew. It would be like old times when my father would throw his head back and laugh along with all the rest. He would laugh at those corny jokes slipped in by the Filipinos as they snipped around your ears and told you about their latest adventures in Yucca Valley where they had a cabin and had to combat goddamn turtles pissing on their hands all the time.

They had this old story about picking up a desert tortoise and the damn thing pissing on their hands as they passed it around, and Mariano, the middle one, the baldheaded one with the frowning forehead, dropping the damn thing in the middle of the road close to nowhere and saying Oh shit fuck he didn't want no goddamn turtle piss on his hands.

"Yucca Valley or no Yucca Valley!" A lot of laughter erupted because it was pretty good.

They told it with a lot of feeling.

How they stumbled across the turtle and approached it was exciting, and all the men sat forward in their chairs, listening with bent heads, inspecting their fingernails as if they had come for a manicure, or they leaned back in their chairs looking up at the ceiling with slight smiles on their faces, taking in this damn story again about the turtle that got them every time.

They always worked it in right about the turtle pissing and Mariano scowling with the damn thing shaking in his hands and Henry cracking up and backing away with Don't give me that fucking turtle! Pissing all over you, man, not me! and Marcello, the biggest, brownest, roundest of the three, as calm in the desert as in the barbershop, adopting the damn thing or something. It was always good for a laugh or two, and I thought about that fucking turtle ruining everybody's day. I was out of the car and walking up to the front door of the barbershop where I knew my father would be waiting for us.

He was there, all right, sitting in a chair kind of apart from everybody. He had his head flush against the wall under one of those palm fans they had put up across their barbershop.

It was a regular barbershop with three chairs, evenly spaced, facing a long mirror that you could see yourself in when you were getting your hair cut, and my father sat across from them at the end.

He barely recognized us, waving a weak hand when we walked in, and my brother said, "You all right, Dad?" or something like that in a casual, easy tone, and of course all the men kind of looked up from their magazines at us walking the length of the barbershop towards my father.

My brother helped him up, and when he got him into his coat even though it wasn't cold or anything, he asked Marcello what we owed him, and Marcello cried, "Paid up! It's been a pleasure, Al!" and he started slapping at his chair holding a bunched-up sheet, waving us away, looking down at the floor where a lot of hair had collected around his wingtips.

"Next!"

So we walked down the sidewalk towards the car, my dad between us but mostly my brother holding him up with his arm around his waist. Then he put him in the car, and this time I sat behind my father, observing his gray hair and the swirl at the crown of his head that just seemed endless.

I settled myself behind him staring out the window at the vacant lot across the street that promised to be developed every year – Coming Soon! Commerce Pet Shop! – but never was, and my brother started the car and rested awhile with his hands in his lap. Then he turned on the radio and adjusted the dial and glanced over his shoulder, tearing into traffic to get us home.

He veered towards the freeway, the short route. It was just a jumper stretch, but the detour signs pointed us away.

"Shit," my brother muttered. He turned off the radio.

So we were driving next to the freeway with the orange signs and arrows around us and my father started crying again, just whimpering into his handkerchief the way he did. He managed to take it out of his pocket and cradle his face in it.

Then I leaned forward and wanted to touch him, but I couldn't. I couldn't put my hand on his shoulder because he was so isolated and alone now.

It seemed like the truth of him. So I just kind of half sat up towards him, watching him cry into his handkerchief. Unable to say a word, my father cried for a long time.

Then my brother said, "Dad, are you all right?"

"¿No, qué piensas tu?" my dad said. "What do you think?"

Then we were silent again in the car, the three of us, cruising alongside the freeway marked Detour, not saying anything, each of us in our separate thoughts, I'm sure, though I'm not sure what my dad was thinking because his faculties were going fast.

He was losing his brain and it was awful and he knew it and nobody could do anything about it, anyway, and he sat in the front seat with a forlorn dignity looking out the window at nothing.

What must have been nothing itself passed gleaming before his very eyes. Brown eyes, my father had, and I wonder what he looked like from up front when he made his way up the sidewalk towards the barbershop. I wonder what he looked like to passersby that day, hobbling up the street towards the open door, the barber pole twirling in the sunlight and the chipped, jagged sidewalk offering no obstacle to him. He conquered it.

He walked on and on up the sidewalk towards the barbershop. He didn't stop but to pause in front of the beauty shop before going on. Then he did something amazing.

He turned around and waved at us as grandly as he could, standing with a kind of smile on his face that we could see from the car parked at the curb. He went inside.

And we sat in silence for a moment. We couldn't find anything to say.

I climbed into the front seat to get on our way, and my brother put the car in drive to pull into traffic.

He let out a low whistle before we merged, and then we ate up the road pointed to Pep Boys. Palm trees reminded me of cemeteries I had passed when I was younger, driving to piano lessons with my father, and a few years later he lay next to the freeway in Rosemead in a bright shiny casket. Mourners dabbed their eyes at the edge of the grave, and my brother coughed into a handkerchief the size of his face, and my sister and mother stood holding each other in black.

I wore my rented suit and joined them in prayer. We moved in a line tossing dirt into the hole, covering the casket with our last offerings. And none of us, really, remembered the great things he had done in his life, like walking to the barbershop on a particularly brutal day to show his boys what a man is made of.

FEEDING THE PEOPLE

Big happenings, big doings occupy my Sunday. Walter Ramirez himself sits on a stool, strumming a few licks, composing a few lyrics to himself as the band scurries around him. The band is made up of two vagrants he's thrust instruments at and told to play, man, play.

And thus he warms up on this fine sunny day in Northern Califas, a day when the sun has peeked out and fooled El Niño of the torrential rains with a dew-bedecked smile. Everything's wet.

His foot is wet bouncing to the beat of his song. The trousers of the players are wet. The equipment is wet.

And if you look high enough up to the warehouse ceiling sheltering Producciones Disturbios, an innovative company spinning revolutionary songs and vibes that doesn't do house parties or weddings, you see the wet spots on the interior roof soaking through. Big, fat drops of rain fall down between riffs, and thus we're called (I'm just the manager) The Wetbacks Extempore. We're jamming and improvising in my studio Number 9, raising the roof in my rocking place that a couple of malcontents have falsely identified as a garage.

"Ladies and gentlemen, a little tune I wrote called 'Helen's Song.' Can you hear me out there? Testing one, two, three."

He starts off with that sad tune he's been toying with all morning, strumming the guitar softly and leaning into the microphone, a doleful expression on his long and tragic Aztec face.

"It goes like this: Helen's song, man," singing, singing, "Helen's song."

"Pick it up," I yell from the side, because I like pace and tempo and none of this revamped "In-a-gadda-da-vida" shit will do for me, even with a Latin backbeat.

"All right, man, all right!" He shouts away from the mic, but we catch it anyway.

Wetback Number 1, Uno, steps into the playing space away from the shadows with his homemade instrument, an assemblage of cat guts and rotted plywood, and sings, "Era la Helen, man, era la Helen."

This vato doesn't really know Spanish, but we picked him up off the street and that should count for something. He spits into the mic, bits of saliva clinging to his bristly mustache, "Era la Helen más fina back in the old days..."

"Back in the old days, see ..." Number 2, Dos, also comes out of the wings and into the center stage space of the well-lit, artfully shadowed studio Number 9. "And we go back, we go way back," he claims into the mic, holding his brass trumpet by his side. Shining below his waist, a belt buckle announces MICHOACAN, followed by a slash and PICO RIVERA, proclaiming his antecedents. He's never been to Mexico himself but carries a thin photo album of all his relatives tucked away in a back pocket, just like a wallet, whenever he goes outside the boundaries of LA. He likes his roots.

The brass trumpet bangs against his thigh, emitting on its own what sounds curiously like a mariachi song. "Era La Helen in the days of su locura, man," he sings into the mic.

"Sí, era La Helen más grande, más loca." Uno backs him up with his enchanted guitar, moving his fingers up and down the frets as if magically charged to produce music against his will.

"We're talking about Helen, man. Saying: Helen's song, man," singing, singing, "Helen's song."

Walter, lead singer for the Extempore, commands the stage like a re-born Morrison. He bursts forth with his tale of two Helens. It is a sad tale, and happy, Walter working it, hushing the pleasantly big crowd in studio Number 9 to a reverent awe.

His band members provide the counterpoint. They steady him with the soft refrain.

"Helen's song, man," singing, singing, "Helen's song."

"It was back in the old days at Bell Gardens Junior High in good ol' LA that I met a girl named Helen Boas, man, and fell in love." He turns around for effect. He wants to know if any of the other musicians have gauged the importance of his statement. He wants affirmation and confirmation.

"¡Sí, cómo no! Go on."

And the beat heats up, a combination of early Santana and a new sound that is powerful. It is utterly Chicano and dystopian. It is discordant and plaintive.

It screeches and pains and soothes and relieves.

"And so that season I fell in love with Helen Boas." Walter shakes his head vigorously, looking very much like a young José Feliciano, head bowed, deep shades covering his tragic eyes, hair flying about. "And all night long we did it!"

"Man, keep it real!" the Wetbacks cry out in unison, attacking the mic together, wanting the truth.

"So, okay, we didn't."

"Helen's song, man," singing, singing, "Helen's song." The Wetbacks jump into action, skipping across the puddles of Rio Grande water spreading on the floor.

"And Helen was a Mexican like us, man," Walter mutters, looking down at his cuffs, soaked to the ankles. "Una chicana de LA. Pero mild, school-bound, fine."

The Wetbacks Extempore follow him with nodding heads. A phantasmic parade of their ancestors fleeing Mexico in the worst days of the Revolution passes before them. Dos, MICHOACAN belt buckle fading and then brightening to PICO RIVERA, screams into the mic, "I ain't no fucking wetback!"

"My people," Uno chimes in, "came here legally in the teens! Across the border they walked!"

"Or took the fucking train!" Dos corroborates as the rising river drenches them.

They stand appalled in mucky brown water.

"Helen's song, man," singing, singing, "Helen's song."

Walter steps forward and proceeds with his canto.

"We're all fucking wetbacks, then and now!"

"Hey! Hey!" The Wetbacks, mightily impressed, shake their heads wildly and play the truth, hard, driving and dissonant. "¡Verdad que sí!"

"We're all fucking wetbacks!" The three bend into the mic in a dirge. "We're all fucking wetbacks! We're all fucking wetbacks!"

"No more fucking pretensions!"

"No more bullshit when we're singing our song."

And they shake their heads in rueful acknowledgment, admitting the sad, wet, and glorious fact that no matter how cleanly they got here, they're all fucking wetbacks. "So I fell in love with this lovely girl."

"Say it, man, say it."

"And we went skating together, man, at the Pico Rivera Rollerdrome."

"I know it, man, I know it."

"And we held hands, man!" Walter throws his head back and sun-smiles at the soggy roof of the studio, mistaken by some for a fucking garage.

"Helen's song, man," singing, singing, "Helen's song."

"Cut it! Cut it! Cut it!" I rush in threatening to pull the plug on all this shit, my disruptive voice providing an arrhythmic overtone jazzing up the piece. But I will only tolerate so much in a song composed and sung on my premises.

"Stick to the fucking story – clean! – or get off the fucking property!" I shout through a bullhorn.

"Helen's song, man," singing, singing, "Helen's song." The band re-groups.

"I was in love," Walter feels it, man, all of it, coming back, "for the first time. I was crazy about a seventh grader named Helen Boas, and she had a sweater, man, a black sweater, a JC Penny cardigan that fit her budding breasts so fine. And she wore it all year long because I lent her that sweater, man, and even though I don't have that sweater no more ..." He leans into the mic from his stool, grabbing the stand, eyes closed, performing, man, performing. "No more, I say no more! Even though I don't have it no more ..." He's an old-time preacher groping for words, searching the ceiling for a heaven so elusive, "If I did, man, if I did ..."

And the band jams hard.

"I would smell it."

"Helen's song, man," singing, singing, "Helen's song."

He sings a song of unrequited love, innocent, hopeful, sweet, heart-breakingly plain and simple.

"And then later, man, and then later …"

Dark shadows cross the lawn of studio Number 9.

"Helen's song, man," singing, singing, "Helen's song."

I prowl around outside. It's wet from the rain but not too bad. The sun is still in the sky, bright eye of the one god we all agree on – don't we? – holding steady with a burning fury that reminds me of the boys inside.

"Sing it, fellas, sing it!" I can't help myself.

These guys are rocking. They're in full swing. My Wetbacks! They've competently acclimated and adjusted. Fully soaked, with Mexico-shaped maps splashed on the backs of their thin t-shirts and huaraches nearly falling apart, they've found a groove astounding to all.

Carlos Santana nods at me from the wings when I walk back into the studio. He gives me a brown *what's happening*, offering me the shake, Chicano style, from the Mission, which I don't know, having learned my shake on the streets of Los. But we work it out. I speak the lingo, though.

"Carlos, man, why don't you move over to Producciones Disturbios," I open.

"Naw, man, I'm pretty wrapped up in my own thing nowadays." He shoots out the door into Santana night, and I'm flooded with excitement remembering his first three albums. Better than anybody since, he fixed the sound of a Chicano soul, plaintive and wailing, beautiful, plangent, and tragic.

"Helen's song, man," singing, singing, "Helen's song."

" 'bout another woman named Helen I heard about in the big, bad Fresno in the not-so-distant past…"

"Otra Helen, man, in the big, bad Fresno."

The Wetbacks Extempore are backing him with a brilliance new to them. Their instruments spark.

They accompany the saddest of tunes.

"About a ruca named Helen…"

"Helen's song, man," singing, singing, "Helen's song."

"Who was so bad, so fine, so lost," the three punch in.

"She was on heroin, man," Walter caps the song.

The two insist: "She was on heroin, man."

The Wetbacks Extempore sing, "Heroin, heroin, heroin," up to the rain-soaked roof, crisscrossed with beams. And then, finding a dry spot, they get down low on their knees and pray to the great unseen God above them, crossing themselves in the Mexican way, blessing themselves.

"Heroin, man, is destroying the people." They implore with fists raised. "Great God in Heaven release us from heroin!"

"And beer!"

"Don't be so severe, ey," Uno responds, a Budweiser at his side. Walter just shakes his head lazily, Jose Feliciano-style. And the two Wetbacks Extempore blaze.

"Helen's song, man," singing, singing, "Helen's song."

"Wrap it up, man, wrap it up, bring it to a close." I step forward out of the shadowy wings, Carlos Santana handkerchief in my pocket, doing a little two-step baile to keep the music going while the spirit's here but wanting to end this song soon and drain my patio.

"Helen's song, man," singing, singing, "Helen's song."

Wetback fans from all over the world might appear on my lawn any minute, cross over the green divide of my waterlogged backyard into the wired sanctum of my music-engineering studio – called a garage by fools – and splash all over the place, ruining my equipment. Plus what would I do with so many to feed?

"Who's gonna feed the multitude, man?"

The Wetbacks Extempore whip around and drown out my improvised line with unaccustomed gusto.

"Helen's song, man," singing, singing, "Helen's song!"

And I back off into the wings again, waiting for this damn thing to end. Haunted by the specter of newly converted Wetback fans converging on my territory and turning my studio into an encampment of taboo exploration, I scoot away trembling, scared, open to but not yet embracing the rawest possibilities.

I want lunch and I want a tight song, man.

"Helen's song, man," singing, singing, "Helen's song."

And together they sing on, Walter center stage, Uno and Dos flanking him, beating rhythm against their knees. Tambourines jangle. Guitars play by themselves, floating in the air above them.

Mexican rhythms roil with Carlos Santana feeds and are influenced by a heavy dose of soulful rock & roll and badass Motown. But then the Chicano/Santana element pierces through, and it's only Walter pacing the stage by himself, holding a microphone to his lips, spinning his song.

"Say it, man, say it," the two Wetbacks encourage him.

And Walter leans down low and spits into the mic, "Was a woman named Helen, was…"

"Yes?"

" … a heroin addict named Helen, was …"

"Yes?"

"… a ruca de aquellas named Helen. I heard her name, oh yes." Walter beseeches God again, grimacing up at the ceiling. "And I saw her!"

"Yes?"

"Walking down the street in Fresno!"

"Yes?"

"And she was wearing garters."

"Yes?"

"And she stank of the devil's rapture."

"Yes?"

"She reeked of sex."

"Yes?"

"And she is all of us here gathered today you me and everyone here gathered today she was and is all of us."

"Amen, brother!"

"Sing it!"

"At the top of yo' lungs!"

"And before we all forget that, oh," Walter drops to one knee and extends a hand to the audience. "Let us beware. For that is our soul at stake, yours, mine and everyone's."

He sweeps across the stage, brushing his fingertips against the extended hands of the gaping crowd. They have appeared out of nowhere, enough Wetback fans to make the biggest rock star envious, crowding in to catch this show.

"And then where would we be, what?" He drops flat on his back and breathes hard.

"If we forgot about our little girlfriend," the two Wetbacks join in, conjuring up a mature and lovely Helen Boas, who walks onstage holding Walter's sweater out to him.

"It's from Helen, man, it's from Helen," they sing.

And he takes that sweater and rocks with it on the bare floor of my studio, crying and smothering himself in its sweet-smelling warmth.

Carlos Santana descends from above. He floats down behind the two Wetbacks jamming away, and starts playing a bittersweet melody like only Carlos can. The two Wetbacks Extempore bow their heads and cry with shoulders shaking.

"Helen's song, man," singing, singing, "Helen's song." And the audience picks up the chant and clasps hands and starts to sway.

I'm running around trying to keep order, though I must admit I'm feeling rather big, positively Bill Grahamish about all the happenings in my space. Neither garage nor studio is my space anymore but something else.

It lifts me in a wave that makes me forget everything.

"And then where would we be now?" Walter fixates on the ceiling, on his back, and, tear-choked and gasping, laughs.

"Who would we be? What kind of people?" He gets up on one knee and faces the audience, slowly rising, tentatively offering the sweater to them.

"This is from my dear sweet Helen," he mouths softly.

"And how 'bout that other Helen, ése?" a woman calls from the audience.

Walter peers into the faces below him and spots a street-ravaged chola appealing to him now. He ignores her and seeks an answer: "What about the question, man, what about the question?"

"Say what?" pops up from the crowd.

"What's gonna happen to us here people if we forget about my Helen? Sweet innocent love and everything beautiful?"

"Helen's song, man," singing, singing, "Helen's song."

Carlos Santana rips loose with an ear-splitting, break-through-the-clouds-to-see-God guitar lick. When he's done, rock & roll is rewritten.

Everybody gets down on one knee and bows. Carlos's licks swirl around them.

Walter says, "Everybody rise," his head still bowed.

Everybody stands. They sway and hum. They hear a soft song.

"Helen's song, man," singing, singing, "Helen's song."

"If we forget her we forget everything. We lose our souls."

"And we can't afford that," the Wetbacks Extempore interject.

La Helen musters enough gumption to show herself. The hardened veterana walks onstage in pale silver khakis and a black tank top.

Walter meets her halfway.

"Helen's Song, man," singing, singing, "Helen's song." It has never sounded better.

The audience sways. The band plays. Santana informs.

Walter and la Helen de Fresno hug on stage. Helen Boas from LA steps aside. And they glance from face to face. Then they all start laughing.

"This is so good," Walter says, "to be here with you."

"Yeah, I remember you, ése," la Helen speaks.

The old chola grabs the mic and looks down. "I remember you good."

"It was so many years ago," Walter raises his hand like a preacher on the circuit, relying on God to save him. Tears, big and hardy, flow steadily down his face. "That I saw you," he continues, "outside the Safeway in Fresno, California."

"I smelled like sex, didn't I, ey?"

"Helen's song, man," singing, singing, "Helen's song."

The people are lost in a rhythmic chant, filled with rapt expectation. A miracle must happen tonight. A transformation of biblical proportions must take place on my stage or I'm out of business and the whole movement is lost.

Santana picks his chords so carefully they're etched in the air. They hang and shudder. The Wetbacks Extempore chase him.

La Helen, speaking deliberately, wields her mic with more confidence now. Helen Boas, always respectful, stands somberly by.

"Helen's song, man," singing, singing, "Helen's song."

"You were there standing outside the market, like wondering what you came for ..."

Uno's cat-gut guitar screeches.

"It was a strange and terrible night." Walter's hands jerk up and hang lifeless.

Santana takes over in a gentler spirit. La Helen watches him and smiles in appreciation. "Carlos, you always made me cry, man, in my worst times. You got me through them."

He nods in sync, eyes closed, sleepily acknowledging her from a far-away place I can only imagine. He drifts into ultimate Santana existence as la Helen zeroes in on Walter.

"And you stood under the lights by the baskets in a real hurry to go in or something."

"Helen's song, man," singing, singing, "Helen's song."

"This is a song about redemption." Walter retakes the stage, gesticulating to the crowd. A microphone hangs around his neck. "It's about goodness and recognizing your rankly inappropriate stink …"

"You dissed me."

"… was not sin but …"

"I asked you for the time and you couldn't even give me the fucking time."

"Helen's song, man," singing, singing, "Helen's song."

"You walked by me like you were some big shit or something."

"I know." He kisses her on the cheek. "Sorry."

"Sorry ain't enough," comes from the audience.

"Helen's song, man," singing, singing, "Helen's song." The crowd wants more.

The two Wetbacks Extempore toss aside their tambourines and stroll across the stage, encumbered with mariachi instruments way too big for them. ¡Híjola! Dos wears the garb of his native Michoacan in loose folds upon him, as if it were skin torn from the body of an enemy. Uno drains a Tecate.

Walter begins to take his clothes off.

"Helen's song, man," singing, singing, "Helen's song."

And the crowd solemnly approaches him.

"Helen's song, man," singing, singing, "Helen's song."

They lift him onto a sacrificial stone and split open his chest.

"Helen's song, man," singing, singing, "Helen's song."

"Stop, stop this bloody shit," I run around screaming to no one in particular. Whoever hears me should just listen. "This is not right, he's a brother, too." But my voice is drowned out in the gnashing of teeth and the terrible sounds of El Niño battering my patio roof.

"Helen's song, man," singing, singing, "Helen's song."

I give up and pause for grace one silent tiny moment before I move in. I devour what's left of our brother and pick my teeth with the rest.

FREDDY FENDER IN COMMERCE

Para Baldemar Huerta
AKA Freddy Fender
RIP

The artist arrived in town. It was Freddy Fender. We didn't see him come in, of course, but I imagine him stepping out of a cab in front of the motel next door to his last gig on his LA tour. It was Salvatore's Restaurant and Lounge in City of Commerce. He tipped the cab driver well because he loved life and people who did their jobs right deserved it. He loved the workers.

Then he stood on the sidewalk for a second checking out the scene. Cars and trucks drove by him on a busy Friday afternoon, no sign of life outside the industry poking up on the outskirts of what must be a residential town, after all, tucked away. He climbed up the stairs and rested in his room after establishing his credentials at the desk.

"I'm Freddy Fender, man, de San Benito, here on a gig." Then he slapped down a credit card and it was gold.

The three of us went to the movies that night, and after we got home, winding off the freeway and entering Commerce, we decided to stay out a bit and have some fun.

"Let's go to Salvatore's, man," one of us said, and the driver pulled into the parking lot with the loose gravel crunching beneath the tires.

So we stood on the sidewalk inspecting the sign. FREDDY FENDER, INTERNATIONAL RECORDING STAR. It was set up on a sandwich board right outside the door. He was smiling in his publicity shot like a Vegas guy, all sparkling teeth and shiny shirt with pointed collar, not like the guy we got to know that night.

So we put him down. "Naw, man, what do we wanna see this fucker for? He's just some country singer from nowhere. *Wasted days and wasted nights*," I mimicked, and the rest laughed.

But we went in anyway. We had nothing better to do.

"Maybe we can get a few drinks." That's if the cool waitress who called us honey was on. She placed coasters on our table and never carded. We'd drink cokes and eat fries if the other one whisked up to us with her pad out, ready to take a food order.

"What'll you have, boys?" is what she said.

The good one came up to us. She got us started.

"And now, ladies and gentlemen, direct from San Benito, Texas, world famous recording star Freddy Fender!" Skinny Paul Martinez from the neighborhood introduced him.

A smattering of applause greeted Freddy. There weren't too many of us in the lounge, and half of us weren't paying attention, more like buying drinks for our mistresses or looking around paranoid hoping not to get thrown out. But we bothered to clap, and Freddy got down.

"Freddy took the stage and got down, man," is how we put it to ourselves later.

"He was wearing that black shirt with rhinestone buttons but he didn't look like no Okie or nothing, just like a dude who's seen some hard times, man, de veras. A tejano, I guess you'd call him, kind of like a cholo but a little country."

"Like an old pachuco, man," one of us said, "with a twang."

We sat in a car in a cul-de-sac, laughing and partying. A joint made the rounds, and bottles clinked under our feet. A neon sign advertised the Commerce Club across the freeway, a blinking ace of spades bringing them in.

"Fucking Freddy, man," one of us said. "Who would have known?"

He gave us a show better than Zeppelin and the Who combined, or any of those big fancy rock stars taking up a stadium and blaring out loud what you can't hear good. He made us listen.

"My name is Freddy Fender and I'm from Taxes," we imitated him when he first spoke. "I'm gonna play you a few of my songs. I hope you like 'em." He struck a chord and had us.

"Man, listen to this dude." We scooted up in the chairs around the candle-lit table in the middle of the bar to watch him more closely. Here was this big, husky Chicano with curly hair, sitting on a low stool behind the microphone set up just right so that you could see his mouth twist and his eyes close when he got into his songs, which were amazing.

"Fucking bad, man, bad."

The Río Grande Valley was where he hailed from. "Down there, en el Valle." He shared more about himself, loosening up between songs and signaling the bartender, jiggling his glass in the air, catching the bartender's eye. The bartender placed a fresh drink at his feet himself, humbly serving this man who was baring his artistic soul.

"That dude had a soul, didn't he?"

"Yeah, he did."

We expressed amazement at the concrete fact of it.

"I'm gonna buy whatever albums he has. Country. Mexican. Tex-Mex. All of them. He's bad."

"Me, too. He's a winner."

"He's a great artist, is what he is."

After his last song shuddered to a close, he set his guitar down on the stand next to him and bowed a little, more like hunching his shoulders and dipping his head forward. "Thank you very much," he spoke into the mic. Then he stood up and turned his back to the audience. He lifted two fingers to the bartender and exited through the service doors into the kitchen.

And we trailed in after him.

"We just kind of followed him in after he threw his arm out and said like come on in."

"'Come on back here, boys, let's have a party,'" someone turned Freddy's thoughts into words for him.

We had all seen it in his face. He wanted to party with us.

"He was lonely." Silence hit the car, an uneasiness growing because nobody admitted to those feelings. And afterwards, when everybody was done rehashing the story, when our own little party was over, we drifted back into our heads and didn't say much more.

They dropped me off at home and I said, "Later, dudes," and they said, "Later," and we didn't talk about it again.

But now we did.

"We did some drinking that night, huh?"

"Man, we did."

"Three dudes from Commerce sitting with Freddy Fender."

"Right there in the back of Salvatore's where the prep cooks cut and shit."

We sat at one of those silver tables where the onions and bell peppers get sliced and diced for the evening meal. If you've ever worked in a restaurant, you know what kind I mean.

Freddy rested his elbows on the tabletop and chain-smoked and yelled out for drinks through the swinging doors to the bar, but respectfully, not like he was a big shot or nothing, trying to prove something.

"He was just cool, man," we agreed.

"We got so fucked up, man. I've never been so drunk in my life."

He kept the drinks coming and coming.

"Scotch on the rocks for him. Gin and tonics for us." But he had been drinking a lot longer than we had, so he was getting plastered, really plastered. "I could tell he was getting too fucked up, man, way too fucked up."

"Hey, boys," he said in his throaty voice, "miren."

He pulled something out of his shirt pocket, an imaginary joint he kept twisting in his fingers, saying: "¿Quién tiene la mota, ése? Where's the good weed around here?" He patted himself down showing everybody he was empty and making a funny face like saying *me no know*.

"Where's the good stuff, ése? Who's got the good stuff?"

He had gotten down on the guitarra for a good two hours, unplugged y todo, and now he craved a small joint to get him through the night and we couldn't do anything for him but cry poor.

"Sorry, Freddy, we ain't got nothing. But we'll go out and get you anything you want, man, anything that you want. Just tell us what."

We sat waiting for him to give us the word.

"Naw, chale," Freddy said. He flung up a hand, not pissed, just giving up on maybe a stupid idea anyway.

He hung his head and his lips moved slowly.

"I been put in the big house, man, in Louisiana, in 1960, for a stick of marijuana. They put me there because I was a Mexican. ¿Comprendes, Mendez?" He scanned us, moving his head in a circle.

"I did two and a half years, three," he rocked himself in the telling, "for a stick of marijuana." He sat straight up and spat the words out. "Mary Jane."

We moved uncomfortably, edging back in our chairs at the silver table with the dishwasher clanging away in the other room. We listened to him singing in Spanish. Freddy's face softened. Then it hardened and almost broke. "En el cárcel, ése, for three fucking years. Three pinche years behind bars like a perro, un animal, que no era."

"We're sorry, Freddie, we didn't know."

He looked up and grunted. "You guys are all right, man, you're my partners."

Then he started warbling, softly at first and then a little louder, "Wasted days and wasted nights …" and laughing a little, everybody loosening up in the kitchen of the restaurant, Freddy with his sad eyes staring at us, me and my friends helping him up and getting him to the motel next door.

LUCKY GUYS

Bright and early in the morning, Manuel tutored me. He unfolded the flag and shook it out, preparing to raise it while I took note. "Do it this way," he urged, speaking around the long rope in his mouth as I crouched next to him ready to pounce when it looked like the corners might touch the ground.

We were standing on a square plot of cement outside the small public library, gauging the wind and distance to go, leaning back and taking in the top of the pole professionally. A frozen eagle threatened to fly away menacingly. As the flag jittered its way up the pole, I relaxed and took a few steps back, off the cement and into the soft lawn behind me.

I shielded my eyes. I watched it scamper up.

"Yup, gotta do this every morning," Manuel reminded me, half-circling the pole with the rope held out. "Boss says we got to, we got to." He moved in suddenly and wrapped the excess rope around his gnarled left hand as he pulled down the freewheeling rope with his right.

The flag ascended proudly. It snapped and fought in the wind.

Across the street another major operation took place. Lucky Guys Burgers prepared to open. This was inconceivable a couple of years ago, and I watched with interest. Everything excited me about this neighborhood. It was my old one and I was up in the morning and, shit, things weren't so bad after all. I was getting along.

I kept forgetting about myself. That was good. About as good as it could get. I touched my forehead quickly but didn't let my hand descend.

I reoccupied myself with the action unfolding across the street. Out of a small window labeled ORDER, a hand darted purposefully, wiped the shiny counter with a rag, and withdrew inside. The small screen slammed shut. A man in a chef's hat moved around in the kitchen. Painted on the smoky dining room window, colorful lettering announced the ongoing special. BREAKFAST TODAY 99¢. I felt a hunger stirring within me, a stomach-grumbling want.

It wouldn't be silenced. But it was too early still to go over there and order. They were never open when you wanted them. You came up to the window at one o'clock in the morning with your pot-smoking pals, very high and merry, pounded the counter and tried to get the Greek's attention for a desperate burger as he cleaned the grill and listened to his music loud, and got instead his finger flung over his shoulder.

"Fuck you. Not tonight, buddy, too late," he explained when you persisted.

"Aw, c'mon, man, we're hungry."

If he was not too advanced in his cleaning he'd slap on patties for you in the corner of the grill. Most of the time the CLOSED sign got hung in your face; the lights were turned down and you and your friends shooed away.

It was a stupid game you played. It was all right. I kicked at the pole.

Manuel let out the rope some and worked it downward in measured jerks. He stood right up against the pole, head tilted back to watch the flag rise. He hummed to himself and commented on his progress as he went along. "Cabrona. Dance for me, baby!"

I ventured out to the sidewalk.

The street was a jungle of activity, cars prowling the early morning lanes, waking it up. Chuck's Bar sat next to Lucky Guys Burgers, taking up half the block. It was a squat building painted a dark mustard color, with iron bars over the lone window; a neon Budweiser sign waited to come on. A sexy waitress offered you drinks on a tray. Lively script dancing on her head proclaimed COCKTAIL HOUR 6-9.

Chuck's Bar was known to be a rough place. Mando Galindo, a hard-hitting fighter with connections to the prison gang with a single initial

– they said he did "work" for them – met his match there. A leather-clad macha biker called him on his shit when he got too funny with her. She invited him into the alley and sliced his cheek before he could get started, smirking at her with his hand to his crotch and grinning at the crowd around them.

"What, I'm going to have to fight a broad now?" He wiped his cheek and the macha flew at him, knocking him down, straddling him with her knife hand going up and down like a weak piston, held back by three dudes keeping it from touching Galindo. When they wrenched him free, he was lucky she was on her bike already, gunning the motor. "You know where to find me, Mando. ¡Con las manfloras!" she screamed at him and nearly ran over him on her way out of the alley.

"Lucky bitch," Mando said, and then laughed. "I guess I got my ass kicked by a broad." He could have killed her if he wasn't caught off-guard with his Mando smirk.

At the other end of the block, wrapping around it in modern brick and glass, an industrial equipment firm showcased its products. Perfect replicas of heavy-duty construction vehicles – high-riding rigs with wrecking balls, and gleaming Caterpillars – shone behind the storefront windows.

The windows stretched from the floor inside to the ceiling in one part, and in another from midway up the rough surface of the wall. They were beautiful, pristine windows. One of my friends threw a rock through the most inviting window once, and nothing happened. We waited across the street behind some bushes, expecting cop cars and fire engines to scream up to it, lights blazing, the silent alarm triggered, and nothing happened.

Lucky Guys started signaling its readiness to do business. The huge stacks coming out of the roof burped smoke. I could almost smell the bacon from here.

"Hey, Manny."

"What?" He was busy wrapping the rope, correctly, in the metal box attached to the pole.

"Ever go to Lucky Guys?"

"All the time, why, you hungry?" He kept working away, singing out his concern.

"¿Tienes hambre? ¿No comiste?"

"Naw, just wondering." I stood behind him watching Old Glory peak.

I stuffed my hands in the back pockets of my jeans, palms out, and walked around the perimeter of the cement plot Manuel was standing on. He was scowling as he forced the last piece of rope into the box.

The flag flapped and settled in the wind.

I halted myself mid-walk and stared out at the street. Heroic images came to mind: I was George Washington crossing the Potomac, hand enfolded in my jacket; a youthful JFK contemplating my future on the beach, wind-tousled hair a handsome feature, Harvard-bound in the fall. I glanced behind me and saw Manuel finish closing the box and snapping a padlock shut on it.

"Okay, let's go," he said.

I skipped up onto the cement plot and hopped down as if leaping across a crevasse. I floated to the truck shimmering white with its faded city logo a faint green blur on the door, enticing me like an urban mirage. I got in through the passenger side in the parking lot. I put my seat belt on.

I breathed heavily. Should I or shouldn't I? It was always so tempting but difficult to do without drawing attention to myself. I didn't want to magnify myself. That's the last thing I wanted, to be known.

Manuel adjusted his outside mirror carefully, reaching out and twisting it; the motor coughed to life and his square-toed work shoe tapped the gas pedal.

I went for it.

I rolled down my window and swung the mirror towards me, as if casually grooming myself, sinking in the seat for a better view. It struck me. I was terrible to look at.

"Ah, shit, man, shit," I muttered. I said it more to myself than aloud.

Staring at myself in the smudged mirror, I knew I would have to get a nose job before my life took off. I was just too damn ugly to get anywhere the way I was.

My nose commended itself to the hall of fame of noses, and not just gargantuan teenage noses containing some hint of proportion but those truly freakish things that appeared in the books of the grotesque. My nose belonged in the manual at the College of Plastic Surgery.

Chapter 1, diagram A. The lowest beings who shouldn't exist.

I felt a sinking in my stomach and a dead weight fall upon me.

I was just too damn fucking ugly for words.

"Hey, chavalo, quit looking at yourself," Manuel said. "You're gonna go blind. It's no good for you. Like those puñetas you do." He made an up-and-down motion with his hand. "Too much playing, not enough work."

"What are you talking about, man, I been working all morning."

"Yeah, on your tan." He started laughing, and so did I.

LUCKY GUYS 2

Let me tell you a little more about Lucky Guys. There's a lot to be said about this place opening up in Commerce, and down the street its competitor languishing when the burger joint of our dreams rose unopposed (finally!) on our resurfaced street. (In the meantime, the Santa Ana winds are raging around us and Manny's fucking around with the flag, already tying the rope in the box attached to the pole, or raising it a bit more, or maybe even stealing the damn thing, who knows? And my old man's lying in bed suffering an unspeakable disease and I'm there in the morning, shit, watching Manny, learning from him, the master-disaster-forecaster himself, Manny de Arizona originally and lately de Commerce: Maintenance Man Supreme. I'm following him around dogging his eminence's trail, sniffing out his expertise. He's keeping me busy, showing me a hundred things to do, "Like this, man. It's easier," most of the time just goofing off himself, finding ways to waste time – time and time again – walking over to his friend Rudy's behind the alley to have an early morning coffee, maybe. Or taking a long shit in the library that he has a key to, using the private bathroom whose woodwork impresses him, after sending me off with the sound advice to be cool, fool, and go have a donut or something from right down the street while he gets out last night's enchiladas in peace. He likes a restful time on the can. Or listening to mariachi music in the pickup parked in the head librarian's slot, sequestered behind the thick shrubbery I hid behind once for fear that the cops would suspect me of triggering the alarm across the street. Or spending time in the library itself with his shoes on the librarian's desk, studying the pictures of her daughters and whistling through his teeth every time he picked up his favorite, the black-haired one with the hint of cleavage. Or he's emptying the trash barrel in the bin in the back, or scratching his ass, pausing for the cause, the main cause, hemorrhoids, as the flag nears the top and he drops the rope and lets the damn thing slide completely to the ground, stooping to pick it up only when he's definitely done scratching and not one minute before.)

Lucky Guys merits a little more attention. As an LA phenomenon usurping the other establishment just up the street, Andy's Super Burgers, knocking it out of the sphere of our existence, so to speak, cultural ties to the east side of LA can be explored, if that turns you on. (It does me.) And the whole greasy, stinking, unhealthy mess served up here on the bun of my choosing, a very sloppy, mismatched bun with overhanging meat and pungent onions sure to disappoint the more refined among you. So be it!

Sharpen that pencil, writer, and show 'em what you got!

Pull up a chair, reader, and absorb yourself in a tale straight from the greater Eastside. Because Andy's Super Burgers thrives in the barrio, be prepared for bad things, wayward hits and senseless locura. Lucky Guys, in the background, shudders.

Andy's Super Burgers merely laughs. (A barrio sneer confirms its evil.) A flamboyant neon sign zigzags into the sky. Under it, everything desirable to a lower-middle-class gastronome offers itself. Hamburgers, fries, pastramis. Onion rings, coleslaw, chilidogs. Shakes, malts (the difference, again?), ice cream-topped sodas and the rest. All clearly priced and spaced on the brightly lit menu above the slathering grill.

The cost? A short trip down Atlantic Boulevard into the heart of Los. Rather, into the fringe of the storied barrio, no less dangerous for its distance from the center. Don't they say those on the outside try hardest to get inside? And the farther away you are, the greater your effort?

So the neighborhood around Andy's bred medium-range cholos, not quite hardened as vatos from, say, the projects near downtown, but crazy enough. And plenty of them as seasoned as any Eastside vatos. Proximity meant shit when you were hungry for recognition.

We braved our way there for our burgers and fries. Intrepid travelers from Commerce drove under the bridge and up the hump of the small hill into the big bad barrio, East Los. We hung out at the patio tables awaiting our orders, shaking our legs nervously, and, when we were hungry, just eating our damn food, bullets welcome so long as we finished our spread before they hit us. "Fuck it, this is great, ha?" we told ourselves, stuffing our faces.

"It sure is, man. Eat it."

As this act opens, be aware of a crippled figure materializing. A cane, and a hand, and my father caught limping onto the stage. It is all dark now, the bright neon sign above – a famously large vertical assemblage of blazing color – blinking off, letter by letter, as a new cast is introduced.

DARK TIMES IN LOS

Principal characters march in. Against the black backdrop, they stand in relief.

Father: a lean troubled man, afflicted with terrible disease

Brother: a chubby handsome guy, goofy and raw, likeable and winsome

Son: an abominably ugly guy, full of self-castigation

Elena Quiñones: a classic ditz and budding neighborhood sexpot

Mother: a demanding, hold-it-together woman of perseverance and dignity

Carload of cholos: the unstable vatos de LA

Greeks: the famed sweaty immigrants serving tasty food to the masses

Sister: a high school prankster, sensible beneath her jokiness

Grandparents: offstage presences of dignity and decency. Muy mexicano

You: an involved reader eating popcorn. Don't smudge my pages!

※

The curtain rises on Atlantic Boulevard at midday, a not too shabby thoroughfare hinting at desperation. Screeching tires and crazy shouting are heard in the distance, getting louder as the source of it all nears. Pan a shiny counter that wraps around Andy's Super Burgers in East LA. The smudged-up counter gleams broadly and invitingly. It sparkles less than a mile from Commerce – depending on where you reside in the Model City – where the proverbially more decent live. They gloat and pretend they are better than their meaner surroundings. Whenever they stop at Andy's, they stand at the counter smugly, glad they don't live here but down the street, theoretically a short jaunt but in reality far away, another world.

Or maybe it's the opposite that they're thinking – they live far enough away but are close in spirit. In either case, they're dependent on me, the omniscient narrator, unseen after this mention. I hover above it all.

A popping sound as of a cork let loose sullies the air. The scene is the counter. A tiny full-headed brunette slaps her butt, keeps her hand in arrested motion, covering her ass. Elena Quiñones falls to the ground in Class-A agony.

"Shit! I been shot!" she screams into the blazing August day, her new ten-speed lying on its side in a pool of light, enough to make anybody sad.

Sister's hand flies to her mouth. "Shit! You been shot!"

She looks around frantically. The Greeks have taken refuge behind a flaming grill. Tongues of fire lick the ceiling and leave black burn marks.

"My friend's been shot!"

Elena, sobbingly up already, twists. She inspects her buns. She cries aloud: "There, on my ass!"

A small tear in her tight-fitting cutoffs offers evidence.

She sobs anew: "I been shot." She is helped by Sister to the nearest patio table where she rests and worries about the availability of paramedics in this part of town.

"Will they come, man? Am I dead?"

"Don't worry, Elena. It's just a BB gun or something. I can see your calzones, man. Sit down again. The hamburger guys are looking at you."

"Hey, over here, miss. Let's check you out."

"I been shot. It's so awful." She limps into the waiting arms of a paternal Greek who turns her around at the counter, and, very gently, probes the hole.

"Yes, you have been shot. Wait here for the ambulance. You want a burger or something while you wait? On the house."

"No, no, I just want to live!" She nearly faints into Sister's arms, a heavy load just conscious enough to loosen her own blouse while being led away. She wants to breathe!

At the picnic table she awaits, with Sister, the coming of the ambulance men. They sit in relative composure.

Meanwhile, inside the car that has carried the crazy shooters around the block onto the main boulevard and past the hamburger joint they love, Andy's Super Burgers, a cackling ensues.

"You got her, ey, right in the ass."

"It was so fine I couldn't help myself, ey. Just popped her, with this." The perpetrator brandishes the weapon that caused the mayhem, a hefty pellet gun with a wooden stock.

"Just aimed and poof!"

"Put that down, ése. Don't be stupid."

"All right, ey. Be cool."

"I'm cool. Are you cool?"

"I'm cool."

"Both of you shut up, ey. You're making me sick. Shooting a broad in the ass. What the fuck's wrong with you?"

"It looked so good, ey. Juicy."

"Check it out, ey. We're on Whittier. We're clear."

"All right, ey. We made it."

Just for the fuck of it, the driver flicks the switch and hops at the stoplight three blocks away. Behind the lean '64 Chevy with the primer spots and new rims, a row of innocuous storefronts looks out mildly and the placid air remains unruffled. Traffic continues at its regular pace.

"I saw them, I saw them!" Sister pipes up when the cops arrive and take down statements.

Officer Zermeño, a stern rookie not to be taken lightly on these streets, scribbles the facts. "We'll look into it."

The Greeks forget how to work. They lose their rhythm.

"So what do you want, girls, a hamburger, fries?"

Paramedics have taken away Elena, providing a girl in distress a comforting shoulder, and, as is required by law, strapping her in before loading the gurney into the ambulance. "Call my mom! Tell her I've been shot but I'm okay! Meet me at the hospital!"

Sister and Beverly, a third girlfriend stuck in the bathroom that day – good thing! It could have been her butt they got! – are left alone at Andy's Super Burgers with a few dollars to split between them. They order a vanilla shake and fries. They need to sit and think.

"Shit, man, we just wanted to go to Atlantic Square," Sister sums up later, ruing the day "and these damn cholos shot Elena in the ass."

"Right in the ass," Beverly stands up and points out the exact spot on her buttocks. "Right here, in the fucking ass!"

It is too much for them to be serious. They start laughing, Sister and Beverly and little brother, too – Son – going over it again in the back yard at home. They are swinging on a bench built by Father years before.

Andy's won't do. People demand a restaurant of their own in Commerce. "A burger place like Andy's, but ours!"

"I don't want to risk my life for a fucking burger!"

They want Lucky Guys! They want freedom in Commerce itself!

"Lucky Guys! Lucky Guys!" Citizens chant at City Council meetings in support of the visionary Greeks – yet more Greeks staking out another hamburger claim in LA! – standing aloof at the dais, as if etherealized into another realm. They propose a new restaurant in the very heart of Commerce.

"Here, in the heart," the older Greek takes up the cause, and indicates the place on the map with a pointer, eliciting a sigh.

"I don't see why not," William "Gilly" Mendoza sings, wearing the famous three-piece that, a generation ago, helped convince a wary populace to incorporate, so statesmanlike was it. "It sounds good to me."

"Me, too!" A usually silent vieja knitting in Council Chambers hardly bothers to look up. "I'm hungry!"

"Passed!" The gavel falls.

"Wait a minute! We haven't heard from everybody yet!"

"Bullshit we haven't! Who doesn't want it? Stand up and be heard!"

"No, no, we've been through this already," Gilly interjects, sparking anew a contentious debate over the proper usage for the property – it's zoned industrial, not residential-retail-industrial, and there are interests, let us say, who would be happier with another ball bearing plant in our city.

But the cry goes up. "No, no, no!" The aroused citizenry choruses and convinces those holdouts standing in the way, those tepid (some say sour) neighbors resisting change of any kind. "You'll see! You'll like it!"

Meanwhile, back on stage one, the scenery has been reshuffled.

The swing bench on the patio is gone. In its place, a convalescent bed absorbs sunlight for a day. Then a neighbor helps Brother and Son wheel it into the house.

The neon sign atop Andy's Super Burgers expires. At midnight, a garish flickering anticipates a final extinguishment. Another day gone, and cholos, partying hard in garages throughout Los, bow their collective heads. They mourn in private their many sins.

For a week, Elena Quiñones hobbles around on a cane, pausing often to wipe her sweaty brow and explain the miseries of taking a pellet in the butt. "It still hurts, man, really!" She laughs less with her friends. She is sad. She is beautiful.

She slaps at them when they tell her to lighten up. "All right, man, shit! In the ass! Enough already with you guys and my butt! Here comes Ronnie. Shut up. I'm hurt."

Brother and Son lift Father out of his wheelchair into the bed, at night, for sleep. "There you go, Dad," Brother says. "Try to get some rest."

"Ay, Alberto, " Mother says. "Duérmete."

Sister and Son stand by solemnly.

The framework for Lucky Guys is erected. Men hammer and saw and place signs warning of danger. A massive billboard invites all to the Grand Opening Gala. Soon the whole city will descend on it.

Grandparents exude strength and character in time of crisis. They see the family through. They retrieve money from ancient shoeboxes climbing the closet walls, coffee cans rusting in the garage, and tight bundles stacked under mattresses. They say, "La vida es algo muy triste a veces."

Son bows his head, never so sure of a sad Mexican world as now.

Lucky Guys attracts with its glossy newness. The people of the town go berserk. They can't get enough Lucky Guys. "The hamburgers, man, have you tried them? They're great!"

"And the pastramis, dude, they're pretty good too."

Everybody is a regular gourmand now. But Son retreats from the frenzy that boils around its doors. He peeks in to check out the scene but quickly decides it isn't for him. People are too happy there, unworried.

Lucky Guys, man. Sit down and have a fucking burger. Maybe you'll see somebody nice there. Go just to go. Do your own unholy Eucharist there. Son engages in an argument with himself, concerning the usefulness of ritual in the present-day situation. An unspecified dementia, rare and horrible, no less so because of its hereditary quality, eats into the life of the family as surely as it devours Father's brain.

Son eases away from people. He spends time alone at the park. He watches baseball games, sitting high in the bleachers, and plunks himself down in one of the bright plastic seats facing the Olympic-sized pool to count the laps of the swim team endlessly flipping. He visits Andy's Super Burgers more than Lucky Guys. He is more comfortable there, less liable to see somebody he knows. He is ashamed of his nose, which is large and growing, an object of ridicule in the neighborhood.

The horror! The horror! The meanness of people comes back to him. A terrible childhood is revived. His ears, which were not only abnormally large but sticking straight out of his head at an acute 90° angle, taught him lessons. He knows what beasts men are, and women no better – worse, he sometimes thinks when striking out with a girl, when catching a titter.

He sits at Andy's Super Burgers, prey to the funks. He eats a burger, fries, the works, washed down by a coke.

More people swarm around him than he cares for, but he doesn't mind in the anonymity of his surroundings. He doesn't know this neighborhood. He just makes a haphazard visit when he gets the urge to sit by himself and eat, something he likes doing these days, eating alone. Without neighbors and friends to impress, he doesn't have to worry about the bother of meeting them. He doesn't have to anticipate hiding himself in some contorted pose, displaying his best side. There is none, really, and he knows it. He is ugly, and it is hard, and it is tough being the son of a man going down fast, with his faculties wasting, and whimpering at night in undisguised pain.

So he sits alone and eats.

Aw, man, what the hell. Grab it. Take the CETA job. Make some money. Plug in.

Son changes daily. He metamorphoses into an accepting guy not wanting unhappiness more than the next guy. He wants happiness, he admits it. Bangs himself up on the job enough times to win a free lunch out of Manny now and then, his friend taking him to the joint across the street from the library. Manny is a repository of 50s wisdom he wants Son to learn. They have even spent the morning looking at pictures of hot rods in a favorite book he has tucked away in the children's section.

His ducktailed decade is the best. That 60s bullshit didn't fly, guy.

"You ready for some comida, man?"

"Vámonos."

They park the truck at Lucky Guys and sit in the tinted dining room sipping large cokes, eating enormous pastrami sandwiches, grunting and pointing at the flag across the way.

They raised it this morning. It is now flapping in the wind.

"Did we do that this morning, chavalo?"

"You the boss, applesauce."

"Now you're learning, guy. You're getting it."

Lucky Guys, man, are you in? Are you down with the program?

Reader is asked to participate with a small rite of atonement. Perhaps he clips a fingernail to the very quick, shaves with a dull razor, or takes a cold bath in the month of March. When that doesn't work, he shakes himself dry and comes to the City of Commerce, exiting the Santa Ana freeway or using one of the industrial bystreets. There he sits in Lucky Guys with welcoming Son.

They break soggy bread together. They sing Lucky Guys to themselves. "Lucky Guys is all right, man, it really is."

Brother appears, a good guy – a basic guy. He does what he is told, which is often smelly and hard. He takes care of Father, and provides Son with a ride around town when he needs one.

Before Lucky Guys and Father's illness, some nights find them at Andy's Super Burgers to pick up a late night burger and fries. They rush the bulging bag home to watch Johnny Carson with Father and Sister joining them. Everybody is up late!

Other times they drive to Andy's Super Burgers and just eat there. They sit among the busted vatos visiting from the apartments behind it, stumbling in drunk or loaded to the gills on heroin, causing a minor ruckus without meaning to. They scatter their change across the counter and slur out their order.

"Give me a burger, ey. I'm hungry. Please."

The Greeks comply with a flaming performance, cooking up a grand meal. And then they all share a table outside in the summer. Everybody falls to it. They open their flimsy wrappers and spread the food on the table, borrowing a neighbor's tray to keep it clean.

"Can I use your tray, man?"

"'stá bien."

And above them, glowing brightly in the sky, Andy's Super Burgers, LA ...